Like It's Christmas

A WINTERSTORM VILLAGE NOVEL

DIANA A. HICKS

HMG, INC.

LIKE IT'S CHRISTMAS

Publishing History

Digital ISBN 978-1-949760-78-1

Paperback ISBN 978-1-949760-81-1

Credits

Cover Designer: The Author Buddy

Recommended Reading Order

Winterstorm Village Series

Like It's Christmas

Christmas Tree Farm

Make You Mine This Christmas

About the Author

Diana A. Hicks is an award-winning author of dark mafia romance and steamy contemporary romance with a heavy dose of suspense.

When Diana is not writing, she enjoys kickboxing, hot yoga, traveling, and indulging in the simple joys of life like wine and chocolate. She lives in Atlanta and loves spending time with her two children and husband.

Check out my bookstore!

Don't forget to sign up to my newsletter to stay up to date on my latest releases, free content, and other book news. Subscribe to my VIP List now!

SINFULLY DARK ROMANCE

CHAPTER 1

Don't You Mean Bah Humbug?

PARKER

"Good morning, Parker." Mrs. Birdwhistle beamed at me as she stepped off the curb to hug me. "Have you heard?"

"Good morning." I shook my head. "Must drink coffee first."

"You kids and your fancy mocha lattes." She waved her hand in dismissal as she tapped on her phone. "See?" She showed me the weather app on the screen. "There's a snowstorm coming. Just in time for Christmas."

"Oh that." I nodded.

"I heard." Mrs. Dankworth waved from her flower shop, carrying a water canteen. "It's going to be the biggest storm. I can't wait." Her eyes softened as if she could already picture the impending nuptials.

The thing about Winterstorm Village was that our blizzards acted sort of like cupids. Mom always used to say that it was Christmas magic that brought couples together. And it was why so many tourists visited our town over the holiday season. It was also why, as the new mayor's chief of public relations, I was determined to make this Christmas the best ever.

"It's going to be the best." I smiled at the white puffy clouds high above us while a chilly wind brushed my cheeks. The Arabelle was my favorite spot in town, especially around this time of year. Our town square was going to look like a snow globe once I was done with it.

"Of course, dear." Mrs. Birdwhistle patted my shoulder, her eyes filled with the same excitement I felt.

"Wait until you see the tree. Rockefeller Center will have nothing on us. The Arabelle is going to be Christmas itself." I was a true believer in "fake it 'til you make it."

Mrs. Birdwhistle and Mrs. Dankworth, aka the town's gossip duo and book club leaders, didn't need to know I had no idea what I was doing. Sure, Mom and Dad were practically Santa and Mrs. Claus. But that didn't mean I could snap my fingers and make Christmas happen. Especially now that the Town's Scrooge was also Deputy Mayor this year.

"Oh, and there it is right now." Mrs. Dankworth pointed toward the skating rink where a red pick-up truck pulled up with a Fraser fir hanging from the back.

That was the wrong tree.

Crap. Crap. Crap.

"I'm late for work. Have a good rest of your day, ladies." I nodded at Mrs. Dankworth then at Mrs. Birdwhistle before I rushed down Main Street toward The Chalet Pastry Shop. With any luck, my friend Briar would be there getting caffeinated before work too.

As soon as I pushed the door open, the smell of snickerdoodle cookies and dark roast made me stop in my tracks. This was the most magical time of the year. Something as small as getting the wrong tree delivered a week before the grand Christmas tree lighting ceremony wasn't a big deal. Who was I kidding? Of course it was a big deal.

Rubbing the side of my face, I scanned the room quickly. Instead of finding Briar, my gaze met Rhett's across the room. I hated his perfect hair, his perfect uber expensive suit, but mostly, I hated that smug smile of his. The guy thought he owned the town. Technically, his family founded Winterstorm Village, but that was over a hundred years ago. These days the Windsors stayed in the big city and pretended our town didn't exist.

Rhett Parker was the new deputy mayor, the town's Scrooge, and as of eleven months ago, a thorn in my side. I swore since Dad took office as mayor; Rhett had done every-thing to basically cancel Christmas.

Taking a deep breath to calm down, I ambled to the counter. I focused on my friend Rowena's serene features and pretended Rhett wasn't there, staring at me like a creep, as if he knew something I didn't. What did he do? Steal my gorgeous Norway Spruce? Why else would we get the wrong Christmas tree delivered?

"Good morning, Parker." Rowena smiled sweetly. "Sam is already working on your usual. Is everything okay?"

"No." I shook my head. "I mean, yeah. I just need to talk to Briar. Has she been by?"

"Yeah. She's in the bathroom. She was excited to be working on the Christmas tree for this weekend's ceremony." Rowena's gaze darted between me and Rhett, who stood a few feet away. "Are you two fighting again?"

"What? Him?" I pointed my thumb at Rhett and leaned on

the counter to turn my back to him. "I barely noticed he was here."

"His face got all angry when you walked in." Sam, Rowena's business partner and barista extraordinaire, joined our little huddle. "What did he do this time?" He set a cup of coffee on the counter.

"Morning, Cruz." Rhett's deep voice sent chills down my spine.

I hated when he called me by my last name, as if we were in the army. Plastering a smile on my face, I turned around. "Morning, Rhett." I knew for a fact he hated his first name. Mostly he hated sharing a name with his father.

He paused for a beat before he reached over and grabbed the coffee off the counter. "I'll see you in the office, Cruz."

I opened my mouth to call him Rhett one more time, but Rowena pulled on my jacket to get me to calm down. "Enough. Let the man be."

"He knows I'm Parker." I pointed at myself. "He does it just to spite me. He's been doing that since high school. You remember?"

"Yes, I remember." Rowena patted my cheek. "Let it go."

"I was Parker until he showed up." I pointed at Sam. He didn't mind that I'd told him the same story a million times since I met him last year. "He didn't want to be called Rhett, so he made everyone call him by his new last name, Parker. I became Parker girl. And he was just Parker."

"So sexist." Sam shook his head. "I still want to lick him though."

"Don't let his pretty face fool you. He's all evil inside." I reached for my cup, but it was gone. "What happened to my peppermint mocha?"

"I put it there." Sam pointed at the mat where three other coffees still hadn't been claimed. "Oh."

"He took it." I pursed my lips.

"I'll make you another one, sweetie."

"No. Leave it. I'm going to be late." I grabbed the black coffee with Parker written on the side. That was his drink. "I need to figure out what's going on with the Christmas tree."

"Oh no. What happened?" Rowena smiled at the door and waved at the newcomer.

"Nothing to worry about." I sipped from my cup and forced myself to swallow the bitter liquid. "I got it all under control." I pointed at Briar who was now on her knees playing with a dog.

"Briar, good morning. I'm so glad I caught you." I pushed off the counter and ambled over to her.

"Yeah, what's up?" She pushed a bunch of unruly curls away from her face as she looked up at me. "Who's a good boy?" She hugged the Golden Retriever who seemed to be super excited to see her.

"Yeah, so the Fraser fir." I pointed toward the Arabelle where the tree was still sitting in her red truck. "That's not the tree I chose."

"Oh, did you not get my email?" She finally let go of the dog to look at me. "I got an email from the mayor asking me to find a different." She cleared her throat. "Cheaper tree."

"Dad would never do that. He knows the Christmas tree lighting is the most important event of the season."

"I still have your Norway Spruce. But you're about five grand short, Parker." She took my hand in hers. "If it were up to me, I would let you have it. But with Dad gone, I'm barely keeping my head above water."

"Omigod. I know. Of course I don't expect you to give us free trees." I ran a hand through my hair. "I will talk to Dad and figure this out."

"Cooper, come on boy." A man in a fancy suit called. As soon as he did, the Golden Retriever by Briar's feet quickly wiggled out of her arms and went to his owner.

"Who's that?" I asked Briar.

"Thor." She rolled her eyes. "Ava's older brother. He was in your graduating class, wasn't he?"

"Oh yeah, wow, I almost didn't recognize him." My gaze darted between Briar's confused look, the dog Cooper, and Thor's stoic face. As much as I wanted to find out what was going on with these two, I had to hustle to the office and see about getting my Norway Spruce back. "I gotta go. I'm already late."

"Yeah, let me know about the Christmas tree."

"Don't sell it." I placed my hands on her shoulders to make her look at me. "Don't sell my tree. I will fix this."

"Yeah, okay." She smiled at me. "Text me."

On my way to city hall, I chugged Rhett's black coffee. By the time I made it to the top floor, I was ready for battle. Dad and I had already discussed the holiday budget. Yeah, it was hefty, but only because the holiday season was our big money-maker. We desperately needed the revenue. The Olde Windsor, our town's iconic clock tower, was in need of major repairs; the elementary school needed a new library, and the public library needed a new roof. Our last mayor wasn't big on maintenance.

I rushed inside, taking my coat off as I walked around my desk. When I went to toss my empty cup in the trash, I found my spearmint mocha cup with Parker written on it already in the bin. I glared at Rhett's closed door at the end of the hallway. "Mother..."

"Parker." Dad's voice boomed from his big corner office. "A word."

"Coming." I set my coat down and quickly changed out of my snow boots into a pair of pumps that matched my pencil skirt and sweater ensemble.

When I turned to head to Dad's office, I bumped into Rhett's big chest. "Jesus." I glared at him.

"He means me." He peered down at me, standing a whole head taller than me.

"I meant both of you," Dad called from across the way.

"Ladies first." I hurried in front of Rhett.

As soon as I rushed into Dad's office, my mood completely changed. Dad was my rock. Since Mom passed away when I was ten years old, Dad was my only family. He beamed at me from behind his desk, and I knew everything would be alright.

"Dad." I went to hug him then kissed his cheek. "You're here early."

"Lots to do, Sugarplum." He patted my hand, then lifted his gaze to look at Rhett. "I thought I heard you out there."

"I leave in the morning. I still have a few items pending before I go." Rhett dipped his head. "Then it's paradise for me."

"What?" The word left my lips before I could stop it. I didn't care if Rhett was going to paradise or whatever.

"Rhett doesn't do Christmas. You know that." Dad chuckled.

"Oh, I know that." I met Rhett's blue gaze. "You're leaving?"

"I'm going to Cancun. I'll be back on the twenty-sixth." He sat on a club chair, unbuttoning his suit jacket.

"But there's so much to do." I couldn't believe he was deserting us in the middle of the holiday season.

"I need a vacation. Cancun is lovely this time of year." He smirked.

"You know what. That's actually better. Now I can do things my way." I hadn't meant to sound so bitter. "Which reminds me." I turned to face Dad. "Why did you tell Briar to get us a cheaper tree."

"Because three-hundred thousand dollars is a lot of money to spend on decorations," Rhett said matter of fact.

Dad released a long breath. "He's right, Parker."

"But Dad, you approved my budget months ago. What did he say to you?" I glared at Rhett.

"We're not the Rockefeller Center, Parker." The fact that Dad was using my name and not his term of endearment for me told me he meant business. "I don't think cutting a few expenses will have an impact on our tourism. Winterstorm Village is magical even without all the wreaths and garlands."

"So what you're cancelling all decorations too?" I threw my arms up in the air. "Just because Scrooge over here doesn't want to spend a dime?"

"It's a bit more than a dime, Cruz," Rhett chimed in.

"Don't." I pursed my lips. This wasn't the time to lose my cool. "Can I see the budget? When were you going to tell me?"

"This morning. We made the revisions last night. That's why I had to call Briar directly. To make sure she didn't bring a Christmas tree we couldn't afford."

"Right." I took the manila folder from him and started reading. They had basically cut my budget to a third of what

Dad had already promised. "A thirty-foot tree is not as magical as a seventy-foot tree. How is this Christmas?"

"Christmas is about friends and family coming together. Not about some fancy tree." Rhett sat back on his chair, looking all smug and pleased with himself.

Bullshit. He hadn't a clue what Christmas was about. He wasn't even going to be here. "Restoring the clock tower was our number one priority, Dad. The clock tower is a symbol of our community. When tourists think of Winterstorm Village, they think of the Olde Windsor, snow-dusted garlands and wreaths." I glanced at Rhett in time to catch his wince. He really hated the Windsor name, but that wasn't my problem. "Tourists come here to get their picture taken with our clock tower," I added when neither Rhett nor Dad showed any sign that they agreed with me.

"It's a make-out spot for teenagers," Rhett mumbled. "The clock is not worth saving. It's too costly. And it has nothing to do with Christmas."

"It has everything to do with Christmas." I pinched the bridge of my nose.

"Let's table that conversation for after the holiday season, Sugarplum," Dad said softly.

"Besides, if we start a restoration program now, it's not going to be ready for the season. That stuff takes years, Cruz." Rhett waved his hand in dismissal.

I scoffed. What was his deal? He was taking his town's Scrooge status to the next level. I continued reading, then finally found some good news. The big gala of the year had not been cut.

"At least we can still have the Sno-Ball." I smiled at Dad.

"What?" Rhett practically jumped out of his seat. In a

single stride, he was beside me reading over my shoulder. "A party? That's a waste of money. Jesus." He folded his arms over his chest, openly glaring at Dad then me.

"Don't you mean Bah Humbug?" I shut the folder.

"You will make this work. I have full confidence in you." Dad beamed at me then gestured toward the door. "Now that it's all been settled. I have work to do."

Literally, nothing had been settled. But this round wasn't over, not by a long shot. "Yeah. Okay." I strode back to my desk while I texted Briar. No Norway Spruce this year.

"Better luck next time, Cruz." Rhett winked at me as he sauntered past.

"You mean, better luck tonight."

He stopped in his tracks, then slowly turned around. "Meaning?"

"Dad is coming over for dinner to help me put up the Christmas lights. It's our tradition." I beamed at him. Did he really think I was going to let this one slide? "Have fun in Cancun."

"Running the city is serious business. You can't change the budget to fit your mood, Plum cakes."

"It's sugarplum." I glared at him, then counted to ten. I couldn't let him get to me. With a half-shrug, I turned to my laptop and typed fast. "We'll see what Dad has to say after his belly is full of pot roast and sweet eggnog."

"Cruz." He stepped toward me. "My recommended budget is based on numbers and statistics. It's a solid plan. We can't run a business with our bellies."

"It's his heart." I met Rhett's gaze. "Dad runs the town with his heart. The people know this. It's why he was elected mayor, instead of you."

His features darkened. Even the blue in his irises went away. Yeah, that had been a tough blow to his ego. Even after he was appointed deputy mayor, he was still bitter about losing the general election against Dad. But this was why he had lost. And he didn't get it. The townspeople didn't care about statistics and solid plans. They cared about community and the magic of the holiday season. He couldn't take that away from us.

"Have it your way, Cruz." He braced a large hand on my desk and leaned in. "But come next year when the library finally crumbles, don't come crying to me." He turned on his heel and stomped back to his office.

I was about to feel bad that I had hit him below the belt, but the instant I caught a whiff of spearmint mocha trailing behind him, I knew that challenging his budget cuts was the right thing to do.

Rhett didn't get Christmas like I did.

CHAPTER 2
Call Rhett

PARKER

"Hey, Joe." I waved at the bartender and owner of the Jolly Wreath Tavern.

"You're late." Joe wiped the counter with wide strokes. "The usual?"

"You're my hero." I placed a hand over my heart.

"You got it." He pushed his sleeves farther up his arms, revealing more of his tattoo sleeve. "Go on. I'll bring it to you."

"Thank you." I beamed at him then made my way toward the back of the room to meet my friends: Rowena, Briar, and Sam.

We had called an emergency meeting to talk about how I was going to make the holiday season extra special with a third of the budget. I had spent the rest of the day running the numbers to figure out which events would have to be canceled. The ugly sweater contest was the first one on the list, then the reindeer 5K, and the free sleigh rides. But I refused to cancel anything. Not until I had a chance to talk to Dad. I had really hoped this year we would have the best Christmas ever. Why did Rhett have to come in and ruin it all? Because he didn't care, of course. He had plans to spend the entire month in some sunny beach.

But he was wrong if he thought I was going to let him mess with my holiday spirit. I took in a deep breath and smiled.

"Parker." Briar pulled out a chair for me, then slapped the seat. "Tell us what happened."

"I'm sorry you didn't get your tree." Rowena reached across the table and squeezed my hand.

"Rhett is a real Scrooge." Sam shook his head. "How can we help, honey?"

"Well." I shot a glance at the bar behind me. Joe had my drink on a tray but had stopped to greet Rhett. "What is he doing here?"

"Looks like he brought a friend too." Briar said dryly. "Thor Walton. The prodigal son has come home."

"That's Ava's older brother Thor?" Rowena leaned in to get a better look.

"Yep." I nodded.

"I thought I recognized him this morning. But I wasn't sure. He's taller." Rowena openly ogled the guy. "And by taller, I mean hotter."

"He looks the same. Just more pompous than usual." Briar rolled her eyes. "But anyway, forget them. Are we really canceling the gingerbread house making contest? I'm so bummed. I had a great idea for it this year."

I waited until Joe set my espresso martini down, then reached for my purse and pulled out my credit card.

Smiling, Joe shook his head. "It's on the house. I heard what happened."

"Thank you." I stood and hugged him.

Across the way, Rhett shot me his usual look of contempt. What was his problem? For all intents and purposes, he had won the budget round. Because of him, we were going to have to rely on more donations and sponsorships.

"How do you stand working with that eye-candy all day?" Sam sipped from his wine glass.

"I don't." I sat and waved my hand in dismissal. "Okay forget him. I need ideas for fundraising. Anything goes."

Rowena tapped her nose. "Hmm. Let me think. You know if it were up to me, I would give you a big donation."

"But we're almost broke. We're hoping to catch up this month." Sam added. "What about a school play? Parents love that stuff. We could charge a hefty price for those tickets."

"Okay. That's what I'm talking about." I squeezed Sam's shoulder. "I need more things like that."

In the next beat, the group erupted with an avalanche of ideas. I grabbed my notebook from my purse and started to jot it all down. The chatting and laughter got louder and louder as Sam, Briar and Rowena came up with crazy plans for making money fast. At some point, I wrote down lumberjack workshops, but then scratched it out and replaced it with croissant baking classes instead.

"You know if we put on *A Christmas Carol*, we already have someone who can play Scrooge." Rowena laughed pointing her thumb toward the bar where Rhett and Thor were still deep in conversation.

"He would be perfect for it." I chuckled. "But he won't be here. He's leaving in the morning."

"Whuuatt?" Sam's eyebrows shot up in surprise. "The hot Scrooge is not even staying for Christmas?"

"Nope." I lifted my glass and sipped.

"Jerk," Briar whisper-shouted.

"I know." I pursed my lips then scribbled a few more notes. "Anyway, I think we have a good start here." I pointed at Sam with my pen. "We'll table the caroling cats for now. I'll talk to Mrs. Birdwhistle. I bet she already has her drama students working on a play. Maybe we can work together."

"She won't say no to you." Briar finished the last of her drink before she said to Sam. "Parker was Mrs. Birdwhistle's teacher's pet all through high school."

"I was not." I rolled my eyes at her.

"You so were."

"I liked her drama class." I shrugged. "She appreciated my efforts."

"Well now your acting might save this town's holiday season." Rowena pushed her chair back. "I have to get going."

"Yeah, me too." I picked up my notebook and stuffed it in my purse. "Dad's coming over to help me decorate the house."

Hanging Christmas lights and putting up the tree were some of my favorite memories of Mom. Though I had to admit, most of my enthusiasm came from the unlimited amount of hot chocolate that I was allowed to drink while helping her. After Mom passed when I was ten, Dad and I kept the tradition going. Unboxing shiny ornaments and drinking too much boozy egg nog made me feel as though Mom was still with us.

"Do you need a ride?" Briar placed her hand on my shoulder.

"No. I'll walk. But thanks."

"Are you sure?" Rowena asked. "It's freezing out there."

"I'll be fine. Go on." I waved them goodbye.

As soon as they left, I got on my phone and texted Dad to

confirm our dinner tonight. He promptly replied with an enthusiastic yes, an exclamation point, and a string of emotes— see no evil monkey, Christmas tree, champagne bottle, and dancing guy. I chuckled at the screen and finished the last of my espresso martini.

Rhett and Thor had already left by the time I ambled out of the bar, which put me in an even better mood. I was ready not to see Rhett for the next three weeks. And now, thanks to my besties, I had a solid plan to make this Christmas the best ever.

I strolled down Main Street, smiling every time a flurry brushed my cheek. In the next few days, the entire town's square would be turned into a winter wonderland. I wanted all the wreaths, garlands and twinkling lights hung and firmly secured before the big storm came through. As I continued down the sidewalk, I made a mental list of what all needed to be done. Maybe Mrs. Dankworth would agree to donate swag to decorate the streetlamp posts.

"Are you insane?" Rhett's deep voice made me stop in my tracks.

When I turned around, I stepped off the curb and lost my balance. "Whoa." My ankle twisted sideways. For a whole beat, I started to fall face first on a pile of black ice. But before I hit the ground, Rhett yanked me toward him like I weighed nothing.

"It's freezing out here. What are you doing out and about?" He squinted at me.

"What are *you* doing out and about?" I shot back then pushed against his chest to free myself.

"I was about to get in my car and drive away." He glared at

me then winced, as if what he had to say next pained him. "I'm taking you home."

"In your dreams. I'm half a mile away." I made to walk around him.

"Get in the car, Cruz." His voice boomed in the empty street. "Now."

I rolled my eyes at him. He had no right to get so bossy with me. For one, we were not in the office. And two, he wasn't my boss. I worked for the mayor, my dad. His smug smile and high-handedness could bite me.

"Good night, Rhett."

"Cruz." He gripped my elbow, and for a split second his eyes softened. "Don't put yourself in danger just to spite me. It's cold and slippery out there."

"Fine." I pulled my arm away. "But only because Dad will be home soon, and I still need to reheat our dinner."

I stomped to his Tesla and climbed in the passenger seat. As he ambled around the car, I realized I was colder than I'd thought. The temperature had dropped significantly since I'd left the bar. Drawing my coat closer to me, I sat there and did my best not to shiver while he drove me home.

The car hadn't even warmed up when he pulled in front of my childhood home. Up until Dad moved to the mayor's mansion, he'd lived here with me. The Craftsman house had belonged to Mom's family. When she passed away, she left it to me. I couldn't imagine living anywhere else but here, surrounded by her books and extensive art collection.

"I'll walk you up."

"I know the way to my own house, Rhett." I pushed the car door open.

Rhett's long legs unfurled out of his EV and climbed out. Fine. Whatever. Who cared if he wanted to play the gentleman. I let him escort me to my front porch as if we'd just gotten back from a date. Before I could fish my keys out of my purse, Dad swung the door opened. "Parker. I was worried. Where have you been?"

"Drinks with my friends." I cocked an eyebrow as I glanced at Rhett. "We had an emergency meeting."

"Thank you for getting my daughter home safe." Dad tipped his head toward Rhett.

"I was half a mile away, Dad." I gestured toward the street. "I was perfectly safe. I don't know why he's even here."

"It was nothing." Rhett offered Dad a kind smile.

"Why don't you join us for dinner? Parker makes a great pot roast. My late wife's recipe. The only way to get it to come out right is to make enough for twelve people." Dad chuckled.

Of course this was exactly what Rhett wanted. The man drove me home so he could weasel his way into our dinner. He was afraid I would get Dad to change his mind about the new budget. I should've known Rhett was up to no good. *Concerned about my safety my ass.*

"Rhett has a plane to catch in the morning. I'm sure he's got a lot of packing to do, Dad. Let's go inside. It's freezing out here." I took Dad's arm and pulled him toward the door. "Safe travels, Rhett."

"She's right. I should go. Mr. Mayor." He nodded once and walked off.

I shut the door closed behind me, then proceeded to take off my boots, coat, hat, mittens, and scarf while Dad looked at me sternly.

"What?" I asked.

"Would it kill you to be nice to him?"

"I'm pretty sure, yeah." I braced my hands on my hips. "Why did you have to make him deputy?"

"Because he was the best candidate for the job. I know you know that." He raised an eyebrow. "I'm going to be sixty-five when my term ends. I can't keep doing this job. I want this town to see that he can do the work as well as me." He tittered. "Maybe even better."

I scoffed. "Don't let his gallant act fool you. He only came over because he thought I was going to use my delicious dinner to woo you into changing your mind about the holiday budget."

"If that was your hope, I'm sorry, Parker. I'm not changing my mind."

"Why not?"

"Because throwing away three-hundred thousand dollars on an extravagant tree and decorations will not bring your mother back." He furrowed his brows.

"That's not..." I stared at him for several beats. "Is that what you think I'm doing? Dad, Christmas and all the events that come with it are about building community. That's what Winterstorm Village is about." I swallowed the lump in my throat. "I know Mom's gone."

Did I feel closer to her this time of year? Yeah sure. But that had nothing to do with this.

"Of course you're right, Sugarplum." Dad wrapped his arm around me and kissed my forehead. "How about you get started on dinner while I work on the Christmas lights?"

"Okay. I left them out this morning." I gestured toward the door. "Don't go up there without me."

"I won't." He beamed at me. "I'll just lay them out. It'll make it easier."

He stepped outside, and I made my way to the kitchen to get the oven going. I placed the pot roast in the oven, tossed a quick salad, then set it aside. As soon as I finished setting up the table, I grabbed my coat and boots and rushed out the door. Flurries flew past me a little harder than before. The storm we were promised was well on its way.

"Dad," I called for him.

"Up here." He dropped an extension cord to my left. "I'm starving. Is dinner ready?"

"Almost." I covered my eyes to look up at him. "I'll come up."

"Before you do, plug us in. It's dark, I'm not sure I got all the hooks done." Dad wiggled the extension cord again.

"Yeah, you missed a couple on the corner over there." I pointed to the far end before I grabbed the end of the cable and ran it along the rail to the electrical outlet on the opposite wall.

The wind blew and muffled Dad's words. His yelp and the loud clank of the ladder falling froze me in place. The next few seconds happened almost in slow-motion, but also superfast. When I reached the other side of the house, he was already on the ground with a big cut across his forehead.

"Dad." I called for him. "Wake up."

"I'm fine, Parker," he mumbled, then made to get up. "Let's go inside."

"Um. Okay. Wait. You shouldn't move, Dad. Let me call 911."

"No, call Rhett."

"Rhett? Rhett's not a doctor. You need a doctor. Don't move." I shot to my feet and ran inside the house to call an ambulance. Even though Dad seemed lucid, he could still have a concussion.

While I gave the operator our information, I scurried around the kitchen, turning off the oven and the stove before heading back out. By the time the ambulance arrived, Dad was unconscious and bleeding quite a lot. In the back of my head, a tiny voice wanted to remind me of what happened the last time I found myself in a hospital. I pushed it aside, refusing to let the intrusive thought in. The last thing we needed was me panicking and losing my shit. Sitting next to Dad in the ambulance, I took his hand in mind and spoke softly to him.

"It's going to be alright."

"I know." He smiled, blinking slow as if he were falling asleep. "Call Rhett."

In under half an hour, Dad was admitted into the emergency room and was being triaged. In the waiting room, my heart beat so fast, it was making me dizzy. The disorientation got so bad; all I could think of was Dad's words to me before he passed out the second time.

Call Rhett.

Dad was right. Rhett needed to know the mayor had suffered an accident. As the deputy mayor, Rhett was now in charge.

With trembling hands, I fished my phone out of the inside pocket of my coat and dialed his number. He answered on the first ring. "Cruz?"

"Rhett, I'm glad I got you." I stifled a sob. I swallowed then continued, "You can't leave town."

CHAPTER 3

News Travel Fast

Parker

"Stay where you are. I'm coming over."

"Where am I gonna go?" I asked, but he had already hung up.

As per usual, my conversation with Rhett was over in under a minute. I had managed to poorly explain to him what had happened with Dad. I vaguely remembered Dad falling off the ladder, the ambulance ride to the hospital, and my conversation with the paramedics.

At some point, Doctor Chen, the ER doctor, came out to explain Dad's injuries. He had a broken leg in two places, a concussion, and a bruised rib. The pain was significant, but she expected Dad to make a full recovery. Problem was, because of his age, she thought it would take at least ten weeks.

The whole ordeal seemed like a bad dream. I paced the length of the waiting room for what felt like hours. On the umpteenth round, I turned around to find Rhett crowding the threshold. He seemed serene and composed. The opposite of how I felt, and probably looked. For no reason at all, I smiled at him.

"I brought you some coffee." He placed it on the coffee table next to me. "I brought it from home. Everything is closed at this hour. How is he doing?"

"They're setting his leg now." Tears brimmed in my eyes. "I haven't heard anything new."

"Hey." He took a single step toward me.

"Parker?" Dr. Chen knocked softly on the waiting room door.

"How is he?" I asked.

"He's going to be fine. He's on his way to his room. I can take you there now." She gestured for me to follow. "I'm Dr. Chen, by the way, Mr. Deputy Mayor." She offered Rhett her hand.

"Nice to meet you." He shook her hand as he fell into step next to her, asking her a bunch of questions.

Numb, I strode to the end of the corridor and stepped into the elevator. To my surprise, Rhett got on as well and stood to the side with his arms crossed over his chest. I couldn't tell if he was here for moral support or as my bodyguard. For reasons I didn't fully understand, I didn't want him to leave.

We walked past two sets of doors, then cut a right at the nurses' station. And there he was, Dad who'd never been sick in his life, lying on a hospital bed with his leg in a full cast and barely awake.

"What's wrong with him?"

"I gave him some heavy pain killers to keep him comfortable. He'll sleep until morning," Doctor Chen explained.

"But he'll make a full recovery. You said that."

"Of course." She smiled at me. "He'll need to slow down

and get as much rest as possible. At his age, broken bones can get complicated."

"Yeah, I'll make sure he stays home and rests." I turned to face Rhett, then did a double take when I saw his assistant Lila standing next to him. "Hi Lila. I didn't know you were coming."

"Um." She cleared her throat as her gaze flicked to Rhett for a second. "I'm here as a witness."

"For what?" I furrowed my brows. I didn't like the way she was looking at Dad, as if he was as good as gone.

"I asked her to join me. Now that we know the mayor is not fit to return to city hall—"

"Are you freaking kidding me?" I whisper-shouted. "Dad's cast is not even set yet and you're already kicking him to the curb? Is that why you came?"

"I came because you called." He stuffed his hands in the pockets of his wool trousers. "I wouldn't be doing my job if I didn't come prepared. Mayor Tony Cruz is not able to fulfill his duties. Surely you can see that." He pointed at Dad.

"Sugarplum, tell your mother to leave that and come help us with these lights," Dad mumbled. "Call your mother. Call Rhett. Rose."

Dad was so high on pain killers; he had no idea where he was or when it was. But that didn't give Rhett the right to barge in here, announcing he was taking over the mayor's office. He had some nerve.

"He's obviously sedated. Give him a day." I ambled toward Dad's bed to block him from Rhett's view. "He needs time to recover. But he'll recover."

"I know. And when he does, he can return to work. Until

then, I'm in charge." He turned to Lila. "Draft a statement to be shared first thing Monday morning."

"Of course, sir." She nodded. "Anything else?"

"That is all." He smiled pleasantly as if he hadn't just kicked Dad to the curb.

Rhett hated Christmas. With Rhett as the new mayor and the boss of everything, I had no shot at getting the new holiday budget revoked, let alone revised. Who knew, maybe now Rhett would propose even more cuts.

My mouth started moving before my brain had any time to think things through. "You know what? Fine." I saw the avalanche of bad ideas storming through my head, but it was like jumping off a cliff. I couldn't stop myself. "You want to be the boss of everything? Have at it. So here's your first order of business...I quit." Crap. What?

"You're being childish, Cruz," he said through gritted teeth.

To his right, Lila took a step back along with Dr. Chen as they exchanged meaningful glances. Neither of them wanted to stand in the line of fire. If he didn't care he was making a scene, neither did I.

"And you're being a jerk." I braced my hands on my hips. "Would it kill you to give Dad a few days to recover?"

"It's going to take much longer than a weekend and you know it." He'd taken two steps toward me and was now standing at his full six-foot-four height. "I'm not the one being stubborn here. We have work to do."

I glared up at him. "Then go do it. Leave."

His blue gaze swept from my eyes, down to my lips, then up again. "Fine."

"Fine." I reached for Dad's hand and turned my back to Rhett.

He mumbled something I didn't quite catch and then he stormed out of the room. I wasn't being stubborn. He was being mean and unfair. Dad wasn't dying. The minute those words flashed in my head, a landslide of forgotten memories flitted through my mind. I pictured Mom in a hospital bed pumped full of drugs to ease her pain and to kill the cancer killing her. The suffering in her eyes was like a punch to the gut. I saw Dad telling ten-year old me that Mom would be home soon.

I had to stop thinking about that. Dad didn't have cancer. People recovered from bruised ribs and broken legs all the time. This was different. Maybe quitting my job had been a good thing. For one, because Dad needed me here. But also, because Rhett had an uncanny ability to put me on edge. Staying away from him while Dad recovered was for the best.

"You did what?" Rowena brusquely set my plate on the bistro table. My muffin toppled over and rolled off the edge. I caught it and put it back. "I quit my job."

"Why?"

"I don't know why." I pressed the heel of my palm to my forehead. "Dad got hurt. Then Rhett swept in like a vulture to take his job. It was too much."

"What happens now?" She lowered herself down to the chair next to mine. "He hates Christmas. I mean, are you still working on all the things we talked about?

"Well, seems now I've gone from having a third of the

Christmas budget to exactly zero dollars of the Christmas budget. I bet he's happy to be rid of me. We never agree on anything." I bit into my blueberry muffin, then took a big gulp of my peppermint mocha. "I'm a complete idiot."

"Go tell him you want your job back," Sam called from behind the espresso machine.

"I said I was an idiot." I shifted my weight to face him. "Not that I had completely lost my mind. Me begging his smug face? Never gonna happen."

"Who said anything about begging. He might not be big on Christmas, but this town is. He's going to have to get with the program. He needs you." Sam cocked his head toward the door. "Incoming."

Rhett sauntered through the door in his usual dark suit and heavy coat. As soon as he stepped inside, his gaze cut to mine. Normally, I would look away. But today, I had no reason to. We weren't campaign adversaries anymore. Or even co-workers. He was the new boss. I was the ex-employee.

"Cruz." He nodded once.

"Rhett," I responded curtly.

"How's Tony doing?" he asked.

Tony? "The mayor is doing much better this morning. I appreciate your concern."

"Glad to hear it." He shifted his attention to Sam.

"What can I get you?" Sam moved over to the till to take his order. While Rhett looked over the blueberry muffins, Sam added, "No Cancun this year, huh?"

"That's right. No Cancun." Rhett nodded. "A large spearmint mocha please."

"Bummer." Sam slanted a glance my way. "How's the

mayor's office treating you?" he asked as he cleared out the espresso machine steamer.

"Great. It's been nice and quiet." Rhett tapped his fingers on the counter.

Outside, Jack, the office intern, stopped in front of the window. As soon as he saw Rhett, pure horror struck his face. All the interns were afraid of Rhett. But before Jack could make a run for it, Mrs. Birdwhistle and her book club ladies surrounded him. I couldn't read their lips, but I knew exactly what they wanted to know. How were the plans for the lighting of the Christmas tree ceremony coming along? According to the mayor's office website, the event was scheduled for this weekend.

The last time I had discussed the ceremony with Dad to finalize some minor details, Rhett had grumpily added how useless it was to spend so much money just to flip a switch. Now that Dad and I were not around, Rhett was free to cancel all events if he wanted to. In truth, the mayor's office wasn't required to do any of it. Technically speaking, Rhett had been right on that fact.

"Hey, did you ever talk to Mrs. Birdwhistle about the school play?" Rowena leaned forward to block my view of Rhett.

"No, I didn't." I released a breath. "With Dad's accident and everything else, I completely forgot. Not that it matters any more. I quit, remember?"

"We'll figure it out. I promise." She rubbed my upper arm. "We can still have a fabulous Christmas, even if the town doesn't look like the North Pole elves escaped and brought their village with them. Hmm?"

"Mr. Mayor." Mrs. Birdwhistle strolled into the bakery and made a bee line for Rhett.

"News travels fast around here." He glanced my way, then turned to face her. "Good morning, Mrs. Birdwhistle."

"Cancun will have to wait. Winterstorm Village comes first." She pointed a finger at him using her best schoolteacher voice.

"Right. No Cancun." Rhett nodded.

"Jack was just telling us how everything is on track for the Christmas tree lighting ceremony. He mentioned there were some exciting changes." She beamed at him. "We can't expect to have a successful holiday season without a proper opening."

"That's what I keep hearing." Rhett lifted his head toward the other five women making their way toward the door. "Sam?" He shifted his body toward the counter. "My order?"

"Just need some chocolate sprinkles..." Sam reached for a shaker.

"That's fine. Leave it." Rhett grabbed the coffee and headed toward the door. "Morning, ladies."

"Mr. Mayor, are you leaving so soon?" Mrs. Garcia intercepted him before he set foot outside. "We were hoping to speak to you about the school play..."

"Later. I'm running late." He fished his phone out of the inside of his coat pocket and placed it to his ear. "Important call." He mouthed.

I met Rowena's gaze. "School play?"

"Yeah, I was going to tell you." She pushed her chair back to grab her drink off the counter. When she returned, she continued, "Mrs. Garcia was in here before school started, getting donuts for her music students. I kind of mentioned it to her." She lowered her voice. "I didn't say anything about the budget. Just that you were thinking about doing a fundraiser."

"Sounds like she told the whole book club." I shot one last glance at Rhett crossing the street with a bunch of women trailing behind him.

"That's a good thing, right?" Rowena asked.

It would be a good thing if I was still working at the mayor's office. But now, I had no right to get involved or have opinions on how things should be done. I glanced over at the book club ladies still chatting in the middle of Arabelle Square. No doubt, they already knew I had quit. News really did travel fast in this town.

Why did I let Rhett get to me like that? Or rather, why did I let my emotions get the best of me? In trying to stick it to Rhett, I'd made things worse for everyone. I could do what Sam suggested and ask for my job back. But what would that even sound like? The mere thought of apologizing to Rhett for my rash behavior made my stomach roll.

"I'm going to have to swallow my pride, aren't I?" I sulked into my blueberry muffin.

"I think so, sweetie." Rowena replaced my empty mug with a fresh mocha. "We can practice if you want."

"Yes." I sat up a little straighter. "That's a good idea."

"Pretend I'm him." Rowena furrowed her brows and crossed her arms.

"That's good." I laughed. "Wow, you nail the grumpy, angry eyes to perfection."

"You need more smolder." Sam leaned over the counter. "And sit up straight. More big dick energy."

"Omigod." I turned to face him. "That's not helping. He's my boss. No dicks."

"Just trying to help." He shrugged. "I wasn't implying anything about his member."

"Okay, let me think." I inhaled. "Rhett. Mr. Mayor. No. Rhett. I'm sorry you acted like a jerk. No, that's not right. I'm sorry you're always a pompous jerk." I released a breath. "That felt good."

"Good God, woman." Sam walked around the bar. "Just say it. Like this...I'm sorry I was a witch with a capital B. I should not have quit when the town needs me the most. I would like my job back." He gestured toward me. "Now you try it."

"Rhett. I'm." I cleared my throat then drank some coffee. "I'm sorry. Can I please have my job back?"

"No." Rowena cocked her eyebrow, then continued in a deep, growly voice. "I like my peace and quiet."

"What is that supposed to mean? I talk too much. That's rich coming from the man who's on the phone. All. Of. The. Time. I sit outside your office. We can all hear you. Your voice travels. Sometimes when I go home and it's finally quiet, I still hear you. You're in my head nonstop." I shot to my feet. "And another thing. The gorgeous winter wonderland design on the town's square right now. That was my idea. You won't survive a day without me."

"Wow, even the fake Rhett rubs you the wrong way." Rowena hid her smile behind her mug. "We have a lot of work to do."

"I know." I plopped myself down. "I hate that he doesn't care. How can he not care? It's Christmas. And now the whole town is counting on him."

"Sam..." Rowena patted my head. "We're going to need another round of blueberry muffins, stat."

CHAPTER 4

Stubborn As All Hell

Rhett

"Why does she have to be so fucking stubborn?" I slammed the door to my office. "We're in the middle of a crisis. And she decides she wants to quit?"

"Are you talking to me?"

I turned around to find my friend Thor sitting on one of the club chairs facing the fireplace. "What the hell? How did you get in?"

"Lila let me in." He shrugged. "Last night, we didn't finish our conversation. I can't leave town before your family matter is resolved. Gretchen, your great-aunt, is very persistent. She won't let this one go, and you know it."

"You already have my answer. It's no. Same as last night." I ambled toward him and sat on the chair next to him. "Kindly relay my message to Aunt Gretchen."

"Now who's being stubborn." Thor shook his head. "Nice digs, by the way. Quite the upgrade."

"It was easier to just move in. Everything is here." I gestured dismissively at Tony's office.

"Or maybe you were hoping one of the interns would run off to tell Parker you moved into her father's corner office." He chuckled.

The thought did cross my mind. I wanted Parker to get so pissed off that I took her father's office that she would barge in and beg me to let her have her job back. And fuck, I needed her to take her damn job back. I had spent all morning yesterday choosing embellishments for swag. Up until this week, I didn't even know what fucking swag was, or the word embellishment.

Truth be told, Parker made this Christmas project look easy. When I accepted her resignation, I didn't think there'd be so much work to do. I had a city to run. I didn't have time for mistletoes sprigs and fake frosted berries.

"She quit just to spite me." I sat back in my chair. "The interns don't have a clue what they're doing."

"So tell her."

"It won't make a difference." I clicked my teeth. "I don't know if you've noticed, but she hates my guts. She literally loves everyone but me."

"You must've done something. She's nice to me." Thor did a double take, then pointed his thumb toward the bar cart. "You're allowed to drink in here?"

"This is Tony Cruz, the town's most beloved mayor." I gestured to the room in general. "He can do whatever the hell he wants. Same as his daughter, Ms. Christmas cheer in a bottle, the town's sweetheart, and fucking thorn in my side."

"This is why I stay in New York, where it's safe." He pushed off the club chair and wandered over to the bar cart.

After going through some of the bottles, he finally settled on a whiskey. He poured two glasses then offered me one.

"I shouldn't be drinking. I still have a full day ahead of me." I took the tumbler and drank. "The Christmas tree lighting ceremony is this weekend, and I'm supposed to read Tony's speech."

"That's rough." He sipped. "Looks like you're going to have to suck it up and apologize to the town's sweetheart."

"I can't do that." I drank some more.

"Why not?"

"Because she's stubborn as all hell." And smart. And beautiful. I knocked back the rest of my whiskey.

"You don't even have to say the words aloud. Just get her some flowers. Write I'm sorry on the card." He made a writing motion. "Then using your most charming voice say, Parker, I would love for you to come back to work."

I chuckled. "The flowers are a nice touch. But that would never work with her."

"Have you tried being nice?"

"Of course I have. She's just prickly all the time." I got up and paced the room. "No, I need to find a way to force her hand."

"Maybe that's the problem. No one likes to be pushed into doing things they don't want. Thought you of all people understood that." He patted me on the back. "Just talk to her." He grabbed his coat off the rack on his way out. "And don't think I'm giving up on your family matter. I'm not leaving town until you say yes." He opened the door and left.

Talk to her. He said that as if I hadn't tried a million times before. Since we were in high school, she took a serious dislike to me. The sentiment grew into something even bigger the day

I announced I was running for mayor, and effectively ruined her dad's perfect record. Not counting last term when he decided to take a break, Tony Cruz had run unopposed for all of his seven terms.

It was high time someone challenged him. Of course, none of it mattered. The town still elected him. Tony won by a landslide, then he appointed me deputy mayor because he wanted all of us to work together. In truth, I couldn't hate the man. He was what this town thought he was—a good man. They needed his leadership and kindness.

What would Tony do in my place? Fuck. He would apologize for letting pragmatism take over and would do anything to get Parker back. I glanced at my watch. There was a good chance she was still at the bakery with her friends. But I couldn't talk to her there. I needed a neutral location, like the hospital.

Without giving it another thought, I grabbed my coat and headed out. If I had to wait for Parker all day in her father's room, so be it. I couldn't let my first act as mayor be to ruin Christmas. As much as I didn't care for all the festivities and traditions, I would be an idiot if I didn't recognize that all those things meant a great deal to this town. As acting mayor, it was my job to make sure the season ran smoothly, and that the small businesses around town got the financial boost Christmas-loving tourists brought in every year.

When I entered the hospital, Doctor Chen greeted me. "Come to check on our patient?"

"How is he doing?"

"Still sleeping. There's no need to worry. He'll be fine." She smiled at me. "I told Parker the same thing."

"She's been by already?"

"She's here now." She grabbed a chart off the nurses' station. "I'll come by in a few minutes."

"Thank you." I nodded once.

I'd hoped I would have more time to figure out what to say to Parker. Flowers didn't seem like such a cheesy idea right about now. I took the elevator, then made my way to Tony's room. As soon as I turned the corner, I spotted Parker sitting by his side.

Last week, I'd accused her of being childish. When it was so easy to see that she was scared to lose the only parent she had left. I knew the feeling well. After we moved to California, I only had Mom. When I was a little boy, I did everything I could to make sure she never left me.

"What do you want?" Parker shot to her feet the second she saw me.

"I don't mean to intrude." I put my arms up in surrender. "Just wanted to make sure you were okay."

"I'm fine. Why wouldn't I be?" Her wet eyelashes brushed her cheeks.

I took in a deep breath and met her gaze. "I'm here to propose a truce. A cease fire, if you will."

"What do you mean?"

"The mayor is still recovering. And we're in the middle of the holidays. Can we not hate each other for a little while? Maybe hold off until New Year's Eve?"

Her hazel eyes went big in surprise as if she never expected me to be capable of a kind gesture. "Oh."

"Let's put all that campaign nonsense behind us."

"You called me a spoiled brat." She walked around the bed, effectively putting her dad between us.

"You called me a rich playboy playing politician." I stuffed my fisted hands in the pockets of my trousers. "You turned the town against me."

"*You* turned the town against you. You told them Christmas was a commercialized tradition that had gotten out of hand in the last few decades."

"Because it has." I ran a hand through my hair. "There are way more important issues to address than who's hosting this year's ugly sweater contest."

"You just don't get it." She shook her head.

When she made to rush past me, I gripped her elbow and pulled her toward me. "Then show me."

Our gazes locked. I opened my mouth to say please help me, but the words didn't come out. If she loved Winterstorm Village so much, I shouldn't have to be begging for help. She wouldn't have quit to begin with.

"Increase my budget by fifty thousand dollars." She glared at my fingers wrapped around her arm, then lifted her chin. "You want my help? I want to know you're committed."

"You're unbelievable." I let her go. "We don't have that kind of money to spend, Cruz."

"It's a sure investment, Rhett. You'll get your money back and then some." She stood her ground.

"Is this why you quit? To force my hand?" I narrowed my eyes at her.

"Of course not. I quit because you are a pompous jerk." She pointed at her dad. "Dad was still unconscious, and you were already thinking of replacing him."

"That wasn't my intent. There's work to be done." I managed to say the last bit in an even tone, though I couldn't help clenching my jaw when her eyes shot daggers at me.

"Well then go do it." She waved a hand toward the door.

"You know what?" I pointed a finger at her. When she slapped it away, I continued, "Have it your way. But when this Christmas goes to shit don't come crying to me. Because I don't care." I straightened my coat and walked off.

Why did I think that an apology would fix anything with her? From now on, I was going to run things my way. As of tonight, Christmas would be canceled. Of course, minus the Christmas tree lighting ceremony. I couldn't risk an uprising in the town square.

BY THE TIME Sunday night rolled around, I was at the end of my rope and hating Parker even more for leaving me hanging like this. Somehow, we had managed to get the Christmas tree up and ready for the big reveal. For the life of me, I had no idea what I would've done if we had gone with a tree twice the size. Parker's project plans were insane. The kind only North Pole elves could pull off.

"Here are your notes." Lila tentatively handed me a bunch of index cards.

"No, I'm doing my own speech."

"Oh, of course. Do you need me to read through it or...?" She trailed off.

"I got it." Despite Parker's accusations, I wasn't a rich playboy playing at being a politician. I did care about my hometown. "Give me a minute. Then make the announcement."

In the crowd, I spotted Parker in her red heavy coat and hat. For a moment, I figured she was here to see me fail. But the energy around her was hard to miss. She was excited to be here, to see her idea come to life. Why did she say no to me?

"And now here's our acting Mayor Rhett Parker to say a few words." Lila beamed in my direction.

The applause roared across the Arabelle and gave me the push I needed to get through my short speech. I strode up to the podium and adjusted the microphone. "Thank you all for being here. I only have a few words. I know you're excited for the big reveal. The last time I was here, my grandfather had the honor of flipping the switch." I pointed at the huge switch in the middle of the stage. "I've had many Christmases since then, but that particular one, I will always carry in my heart. All that to say, it's good to be home." I gestured toward Aunt Gretchen. "Which is why I have invited my grandfather's sister to carry on Winterstorm Village's most beloved tradition tonight and do the honors." I nodded at her.

She smiled gently at me, looking prouder than she should be. She gave the crowd another moment to cheer until the excitement and anticipation crackled in the air. I'd be lying if I said I wasn't enjoying this moment. I glanced over at Parker and her red cheeks. She was like a child in a candy store.

When the multi-colored lights came on, there was a moment of complete silence, as if the entire town had gone breathless for a beat. Then, clapping and whistling erupted as the high school band marched on stage, playing a Christmas tune while the fireworks painted the dark sky with even more sparkling lights. I stood there smiling at the display. For the first time in a long time, Christmas didn't hurt.

My gaze found Parker again. To my surprise, she was looking straight at me. She was pleased with me. Another first.

I nodded once. And she returned the gesture with a blinding smile.

As soon as the band finished their second piece, I spoke into the mic again and thanked everyone for attending the ceremony. Now that the officially lit Christmas tree stood tall and proud, everyone dispersed quickly to browse the different tents the local stores had set up to sell their wares. Except for Parker. She stood there with teary eyes, while she beamed at the glittering tree.

"Come hug your great-aunt, Rhett. You might not consider yourself a Windsor anymore, but I'm still family." Aunt Gretchen opened her arms.

"Thanks for making the trip up." I hugged her and kissed both of her cheeks. "I thought after Thor gave you my message, you would not think the trip was worth your time."

"It was well worth my time." She smiled at me proudly. "Your grandfather would've been pleased to see you here tonight." She patted my chest. "Join me for dinner."

"You're not going back to the city tonight?"

"No, I decided to stay. Big storm coming. I'd rather not deal with it." She waved her hand in dismissal. "Dinner?"

"Is Thor coming?" I offered her my arm and escorted her down the steps.

"How about we give our family business a rest for a little while?" She winked at me. "I'll call my driver."

Aunt Gretchen released my arm to rummage through her purse. I glanced around as the wind picked up around us.

"All set." Aunt Gretchen reached for my arm again.

"Yeah, let's get out of here. The temperature just dropped." I escorted her through the dwindling crowd. Before we reached the end of the street, the snow began to fall, and the wind picked up with a loud whistle. The storm we were expecting tomorrow was already here.

"Aunt Gretchen, I'm going to have to bail on dinner." I pulled her toward her limo.

"That wretched storm is early, isn't it? Go, Mr. Mayor. I can find my driver from here." She hugged me tight. "This doesn't mean you're off the hook for dinner. I'll be calling on you soon."

"I'm well aware. There's Louis now." I held her hand and ushered her to her car.

I waited until the car turned off Main Street to scan the crowd, looking for Parker. She couldn't have gone far. I'd seen her just a few minutes ago. I stopped Lila as she rushed by me. "Have you seen Parker?"

"She was by the stage." She shielded her eyes from the snow flurries. "I think she left."

"Do you need a ride home?" I asked her.

"I'm fine. My friends are waiting." She pulled her coat tighter around her. "Go home, Boss."

"Yeah. Be safe." I darted toward my car, hoping Parker didn't think it would be a good idea to walk home from here.

As soon as I climbed in, I called dispatch and asked them to sound the alarm and warn the townspeople to seek shelter. Just fucking great. The week I took over as Mayor, I got stuck with a major holiday event and a severe snowstorm.

By the looks of it, the weather system was right. This storm was going to be the mother of all blizzards.

Be careful what you wish for.

CHAPTER 5

Let's Fake It

Parker

"Thank you for letting us crash at your place." Rowena set her overnight bag on the floor near the door. "I'm so getting my generator replaced this week. I don't know why I didn't do it over the summer."

"I was glad for the company. Doctor Chen wanted to keep Dad in the hospital until the snowstorm was over." I set a plate of pancakes on the kitchen counter.

Sam immediately grabbed a plate and piled it high before adding a hefty swirl of maple syrup. "My generator was fine. But there was no way I was going to miss a sleepover. How's your dad doing?"

"He's fine. Awake. But still a bit weak. I'm hoping he can come home soon."

"What matters is that he's fine. And that our new hot mayor is handling himself well." Sam sipped from his cup of coffee. "You have to admit. The Christmas tree lighting ceremony was impressive."

"Yeah, it was magical. Well, until the blizzard hit us." I took the bar stool next to him while he poured more coffee into three mugs. "And now that the roads are clear, I have to go do the thing."

"Yes, you have to do the thing." Rowena popped a strawberry in her mouth. "You're not allowed to come back without your job."

The three of us had been stuck at home for the last three days while the crews worked hard to clear the streets. Most parts of town had been without electricity, half buried in snow. According to the news, all roads in and out of Winterstorm Village were completely blocked and would remain that way for at least another week.

"Don't worry about us. We'll clean up." Sam cocked an eyebrow. "I've seen you scarf down a blueberry muffin in ten seconds flat. You're stalling."

"I'm not." I glanced down at my plate. Crap I was.

"Just like we practiced." Rowena squeezed my hand, then leaned forward to cut up my pancake into small squares the way Mom used to do it.

"Mr. Acting Mayor," I said in a serious tone.

"Just Mayor." Sam pinched the bridge of his nose. "Let it go, Parker. He's doing good work."

"Right. I know. Force of habit." I pierced a piece of pancake drenched in maple syrup and popped it in my mouth. "Mr. Mayor, I would like to apologize for my rash behavior. Can I have my job back. Please."

"She's got it." Rowena beamed at me.

"Hmm." Sam took a long sip of coffee. "It'll have to do."

After I finished my breakfast, I got dressed and headed out to find Rhett. Last I heard from Jack, he'd mentioned Rhett had been at city hall during and after the storm. I had been a real jerk for not accepting his call for a cease-fire. Knowing his big ego, I knew it took a lot for him to be able to say the words aloud. Why did I have to get greedy and ask for more city funds?

Well, it was as Rowena had said. It wasn't too late to fix it. We still had three weeks before Christmas Eve, which was the night of the Sno-Ball. We had time to turn things around. Especially now that Rhett seemed to be on-board with going big with our Christmas plans.

I turned the corner on Main Street, and my heart sank. I knew there had been some damage to the town square due to high wind speeds, but I hadn't expected the Christmas tree to be belly up and for the Olde Windsor to be practically a pile of bricks. Damn it. We needed something big to turn this holiday season around. Something bigger than a gingerbread house making contest.

"It's a shame, Parker. Isn't it?" Mrs. Dankworth cradled a piece of rock to her body. "A keepsake," she explained.

"What? No. You can't take pieces of the clock tower. We're going to fix it. All of it." I gestured in the general direction of the Arabelle.

"I know you will, sweetie. But I just don't see how all of this can be restored by Christmas."

"Don't worry, Mrs. Dankworth. Now that the streets are clear, we're working on a solution." I smiled. "A few days tops."

"I sure hope so." She shook her head. "The book club ladies are talking about canceling Christmas. The mayor told them Cancun was amazing this time of year. Now they want to go check it out."

"What? No, they can't do that." I stood there, staring at the devastation the blizzard had left behind. "Tell them Rhett and I have big plans."

"I thought you had quit."

"Nope. I mean, yeah, Rhett and I got into a tiny little fight. So tiny. But I'm still very much in charge of Christmas." I lied through my teeth.

"That's not what I heard, dear." The pity in her eyes cut me.

"Tell your book club to stay put. We're going to turn this around. I promise." I glanced down at my watch. "I'm late for work. Have a good day."

"You too, sweetie." Mrs. Dankworth blew out a deflated breath.

I speed-walked to city hall on the other end of the town square and marched straight into Rhett's office. "Rhett," I called out.

But his office was empty. Back in the bullpen, a sleepy Jack holding a cup of coffee greeted me. "Morning."

"Have you seen Rhett? I mean, the mayor."

"Yeah, he's in his office."

"No, I was just there." I pointed behind me.

"Oh." He suddenly looked wide awake. "His other office?"

"What? I know he didn't take over my father's things." I stormed to the opposite end of the room with Dad's door in my line of sight.

"He is the mayor, Parker." Jack called after me.

I didn't even think to knock. Instead, I barged in. "How dare you?"

"Excuse me?" A shirtless Rhett stood in the middle of the room looking at me like I was some sort of peeping Tom.

"Omigod." I spun around and covered my eyes. "Why are you naked in Dad's office?"

"First of all, as acting mayor, this is my office. And second of all, I'm not naked. I spilled coffee. I'm changing into a fresh dress shirt. Try knocking next time."

"Please just cover up. Throw a sheet over your head or something." I glanced upward and tried not to picture the glorious set of abs I'd just seen. Or did I make that up? No way Rhett was that crazy hot underneath his fancy suits. "Are you decent now?"

"Oh shit." He clicked his teeth. "Now my pants fell off."

"What?" I turned around to find a fully clothed Rhett, with an amused smile on his face. I narrowed my eyes at him. "You're a child."

"You're too easy." He chuckled.

"You're in a surprisingly good mood." I gestured toward the window and all the winter fuckery going on in the town's square. "You know considering the Arabelle is still in shambles."

"If you'd walked in five minutes earlier, you would've found a completely different scenario."

"That would've been preferable. Now I have to go home and wash my eyes with soap." I threw that in to make it clear that I didn't find him attractive in the least.

"Yeah, okay, good luck with that." He flashed me a smug smile. "Anyway, just heard some good news. The guys have assured me they're on track to have it all restored by end of day tomorrow." He let out a sigh. "Chaos, I can handle. Christmas? Not so much." He ambled toward the floor-to-ceiling windows, looking very much like he belonged in this space, as if he was always meant to be mayor. "How's this for a magical blizzard? What's the town's motto?" He turned to me.

"Love is always in the air at Winterstorm Village during the holidays." I recited from memory. "Apparently people fall in love every time a good blizzard hits town. It's just a slogan, Rhett." I shrugged.

"It's stupid." He braced his hands on his hips. "People want magic. I can't do that. Impeccable emergency response is more my thing." He waved in the general direction of the Arabelle.

"I get what you mean." I joined him by the window. "The book club ladies are talking about canceling Christmas. Some ONE told them Cancun was awesome this time of year."

"You can't cancel Christmas." He met my gaze. "It comes every year whether you like it or not. No matter how hard you try. Trust me, I've tried."

"Bah Humbug." I said in a fake baritone voice.

"What?" He furrowed his brows at me.

"Every time you talk about Christmas, that's all I hear in my head. You're like a real-life Scrooge." Crap. That was not why I was here. I had to focus and get my damn job back. "I'm sorry."

"Hmm?" He leaned in, cocking his head. "I didn't quite catch that. What?"

I rolled my eyes. "I said...I am sorry."

"Not sure what for, but I'll take it."

I exhaled. "I should've accepted your cease-fire treaty. Back at the hospital. If your offer still stands, I would like to humbly accept."

"Wow. And you said all that with a straight face. Did it hurt?" he teased.

"A little. Actually, I'm feeling a little nauseous." I met his gaze just as a ray of light slanted across the room. He had the bluest eyes. Smoldering, Sam had called Rhett's overall energy. I saw it now. "Is that a yes? Can I have my job back?"

"Yes, Cruz. You can have your job back."

"Thank you, Rhett." I sighed. "I really didn't want to tell Dad I had quit."

"Me neither." He winked.

"You saw him?"

"Yeah, this morning. I needed some advice." He ran a hand through his perfectly-styled hair. "I don't know what this town wants from me."

"What did Dad say?"

"He said they needed magic." He scoffed. "What the hell does that even mean?"

I thought of Mom and all her elaborate schemes to make me believe in the magic of Christmas—how she would talk Dad into dressing up as Santa to deliver presents right at midnight, the Christmas trees she would set up on our front porch and all over the house, and all the food she would pretty much start cooking at the beginning of the month. She surrounded us with traditions and family time. Through the years, all of that combined somehow amounted to what now felt as magical Christmases with Mom.

Altogether, Dad had been Mayor of Winterstorm Village for twenty-our years. The town was known for its traditions and lavish holiday celebrations because he made it happen. That was what the people needed—an excuse to build community, to make memories, and to be merry.

As it always happened with some of my worst ideas, my

mouth started moving before my brain had had time to fully process the thought. "Fake it 'til you make it."

"You can't fake running a town, Cruz," he said dryly.

"I know." I put up my hands. "But hear me out. Crap. I can't believe I'm going to say this. Okay. You know our town slogan."

"Yeah, love is always in the air." He rolled his eyes.

"This past blizzard—" I pointed at the Arabelle. "—Is the biggest we've ever seen."

"No." He cocked an eyebrow.

"Yeah, it is."

"I mean." He put up his index finger and drew a circle near the top of my head. "No to whatever you're thinking."

"You're thinking it too." I slapped his hand away. "It's a sign. We've never agreed on anything. Just for that it has to work. The math is easy. Blizzard equals love. Love equals magic." I paced up and down his office for a few rounds while the idea gelled in my head. "The traditions and slogan of our town are already in place. All we have to do is lean into it."

"Lean into it? You mean lie? Because I'm pretty sure no one has fallen in love in the past three days since the snowstorm hit."

"Not just any one. I mean us. Let's fake it." I beamed at him. "It's perfect. Nothing shy of pure magic could get the two of us to fall in love. Come on. You gotta admit that's brilliant."

"The whole town knows we've been rivals for years. And I mean, that scene at the hospital. That was cutthroat." He said mostly to himself.

"Which time?"

"The first one. When we had witnesses." He waved his hand in dismissal.

I could almost see the wheels turning in his head.

After a few moments of mulling it over, he finally looked up at me. "Cruz, this idea of yours might just work."

"It will work." I darted to his desk and picked up a pad. "We need a schedule. First, we need to leak the information. People love secrets. It'll make it more believable if the whole town thinks we've been hiding our love."

"Our lo..." He rubbed the side of his face. "It's scary how quickly you came up with this whole scheme."

"Shhh. Let me think." I jotted down a few ideas for first dates. "Are you free tomorrow around two?"

"Why?"

"How do you feel about croissant baking classes? Romantic, or no? Maybe something more public?"

"Why?" he asked again, a little slower this time.

"For our first date. We'll drink some hot chocolate, eat cookies, SKATING." My hand could barely keep up with my brain as I scribbled on the page.

"Jesus, a date?" Rhett reached over and yanked the pen out of my hand.

"Hey." I turned to glare at him.

"You need to slow down." He tossed the pen over his shoulder. "What are you going to do when people want us to kiss?"

"Why would they even ask? That would be creepy. Relax, it'll never come to that. At most, we'll have to hold hands." I stopped to inhale and give him a chance to catch up.

He rubbed the creases on his forehead as he paced to the fireplace and back. Every time, he glanced up at me, his intense gaze would settle on mine. He was really considering all the angles. How about that? We actually made a good team. I was the idea instigator. He was the executor.

"Proximity." He finally said.

"What does that mean?"

"Can you handle it?" He cocked his head.

"What?"

He prowled toward me as his eyes darkened. Was he mad now? No, that wasn't it. Rhett was doing the smoldering thing on me. Shit, I swallowed to ease my dry throat. Okay, I could do this. I was a professional. He stopped a mere two inches from me. We'd never been this close before. Oddly enough, I wasn't repulsed by it. It was nice.

"I'm not nauseous." I lifted my head to look at him. "You?"

His jaw clenched then released, his gaze never leaving mine... "It's doable." He nodded then reached behind me.

I glanced over my shoulder and followed his line of sight. "What are you doing?" I asked when he pressed the intercom button.

"Lila, can I see you in my office, please." He released the button and turned to me. "Getting the ball rolling."

"Lila is Mrs. Birdwhistle's god daughter. She'll be Lila's first call. And then..."

"And then, the whole town will know." He brought his hand up to my waist. "Last call to back out, Cruz. It's now or never."

"Never." I placed my hand on his chest just as he leaned in to press his forehead to mine.

My heart drummed so hard, I swore I heard its echo against the walls. Once Lila barged in on us, we would have to follow through on our lie, all the way to New Year's Eve. How hard could it be?

"Omigod." Lila dropped her iPad. "I'm sorry." She bent down to retrieve it then fell to her knees while trying to reach for her Mac pen. "I'm sorry. I didn't mean to...um, the door was opened."

"It's fine. I was just leaving." I tentatively stepped away from Rhett. I hadn't considered how much touching we needed to do to convey our message. As it was, it already felt like I'd been in Rhett's arms for a very long time.

For his part, Rhett slowly released my waist and let his fingers skim the length of my arm until they landed in my palm. Our bodies moved with such synchronicity, I didn't have time to react to the goosebumps fluttering my skin or jerk away from him. I just stood there, spellbound.

Lila's eyes widened as she focused on our intertwined hands. "No. I'll come back. My phone is ringing." She shut the door behind her.

"And we're off." Rhett let go of me, sauntered around his desk, then sat. "Can you stay the rest of the day? We're buried in work. I could use the help."

"Um. Yeah. Yeah, I can do that." I took in a deep breath while I re-oriented myself. "I'll just um, I'll go back to my desk."

"Thanks. Can you send Lila in? I do need talk to her." He chuckled.

"Yeah." I studied my fisted hand for a moment before I shifted my attention back to him. "I'll give her another minute to make that call to Mrs. Birdwhistle."

"Good thinking, Cruz."

Yeah, as far as crazy ideas went, fake dating my new grumpy boss was the worst of them all. Too late to back down now though. If Rhett could play his part, I could too.

CHAPTER 6

I Rarely Think of You

PARKER

"Are you sure you're okay?" Briar escorted me to my front door, but then wiggled away from me. "You're acting weird."

"What? No, I'm not." I scoffed, stuffing my hands in the pockets of my hoodie.

If I didn't get rid of Briar in the next five minutes, I was going to be late to my first fake date with Rhett. As it was, I barely had half an hour to get ready. And I had zero idea what to wear or what to expect.

Yesterday morning after we agreed to this crazy plan to pretend we were in love to restore the town's holiday spirit, we didn't really get a chance to hash out the details. Throughout the day, I'd tried to talk to him, but the fake dating gods weren't on our side. While I caught up on emails, Rhett worked with his emergency and restoration teams to get Winterstorm Village back in business. I left work fairly late, and he was still holed up in his office, holding some kind of project status meeting.

The more I thought about it, the more I realized, we needed ground rules, a plan for telling our friends and family. They were going to demand details on how we got together. And more importantly, they would want to know why, after so many years, we decided to fall in love. Sure, the town would blame it on the magical storm. But Rowena, Sam and Briar would never let me off the hook that easily.

And what about Dad? Oh crap. How in the world was I going to tell Dad about Rhett? Would he be encouraging? He did, after all, ask me to be nicer to Rhett. Dating him counted as being nicer? Right?

"I know you." Briar cocked her head to look me in the eye. "You're up to something."

"I just have a lot going on at work. The Sno-Ball is in three weeks; we have the school play before that. The blizzard really set us back." I stopped talking when she beamed at me.

"You got your job back?" She hugged me. "That's great. I knew Rhett would reconsider."

"Yeah, he did." I fisted my hand as a tingly sensation ran from my elbow to my wrist. Just like it'd happened yesterday when Rhett brushed his fingers across my arm and a trail of goosebumps fluttered on my skin. "We called a truce."

"That's great news." She shot a glance toward the door. "I should go. You probably have a million things to do for the Sno-Ball."

"I do. But it was great seeing you. I'm glad your generator is back in business. I wish I had known you were in trouble."

As it turned out, while Rowena, Sam and I were enjoying our girls' night in, Briar was at her Christmas tree farm with no electricity and no way to get to us or call for help.

"I feel terrible. I should've checked on you after that first night. I hate that you were all alone."

"Um. Yes. I was alone." She crossed her arms over her chest the way she always did when she lied.

Briar Storey was up to something. I narrowed my eyes at her. Now who was acting weird? What really happened to her during the snowstorm? Whatever it was, it would have to wait. If she was lying or not, I had no time to prod.

She glanced down at her hands, then uncrossed her arms. "I mean, you had no way of knowing I was all alone with no power. I really was fine when you called. Until I wasn't." Her cheeks turned a bright red. "Enough about that." She gestured toward the door. "I'll see you later."

"Yeah." I side-stepped her and opened the door.

A gust of wind rushed through the house. When it settled, Rhett appeared on my front porch with a gorgeous floral bouquet in his hands. Oh crap. I stood there as my gaze shifted between a very confused Briar and a dashing Rhett, who didn't seem fazed at all. Me on the other hand? I froze, deer-in-headlights style.

"Mr. Mayor. What a happy coincidence." Briar gave me a meaningful look. "Come in. It's chilly out there."

"Thanks." Rhett entered my house for the first time ever and set the flowers on the dining room table to his left.

"It was good to see you." She gave me another quick hug, then whispered in my ear, "We're so talking about this later." When she pulled back, she waved at Rhett, then me. "I'll leave you two to it."

As soon as the door shut, Rhett released a breath. "We didn't exactly discuss what we're telling our friends."

"Yeah, I didn't think about that." I shook my head. "I mean I did. But you were so busy yesterday."

"I meant to call you, but it was midnight by the time I had a free moment." He surveyed my face.

Suddenly, there was an electric charge between us. The idea of Rhett thinking about calling me in the middle of the night felt way too intimate. My arm tingled again, and I had to shake my head to snap out of it.

"Flowers? You know that this isn't a real date, right?" I pointed at the dining table.

"Oh." He furrowed his brows. "Mrs. Dankworth made me buy them for you. Of course, Mrs. Birdwhistle called her immediately just like you said. Anyway, she practically corralled me into her shop and showed me your favorite flowers."

"They're gorgeous. And yea, red roses are my favorite. I know. So, cliché, huh?" I stuffed my hands in the pockets of my hoodie then stopped. Crap. I glanced down at my fuzzy socks and my sweatpants, then up to look at Rhett and his perfectly put together ensemble. In his jeans, cashmere sweater, and heavy coat, he was the epitome of a hot date. And why did he have to smell so good for a pretend date? "I need a few minutes to get ready."

"Of course." He smiled. "Take your time."

"Okay." I winced. Did I want to leave Rhett alone in my kitchen while I got ready? I didn't need my office nemesis snooping around my stuff. Sure, we had called a cease-fire, but that didn't mean I could trust him. "Um."

"Don't worry, Cruz. I'm not here to steal any political secrets. We're on the same team now, remember?" He sauntered down the hallway to the living room and removed his coat.

"Okay. Can I get you anything to drink?" I ambled to the open-concept kitchen.

"I'll take a glass of wine if you have it." He turned to face me.

I didn't like that he felt so comfortable in my home. "We need a better plan than letting Mrs. Birdwhistle spread rumors on our behalf." I strode to the wine fridge and grabbed a 2015 Chateauneuf du Pape. Not that I wanted to impress him, I simply needed good red wine to get through today's crazy date —fake date. "We should tell my friends the truth." I set two glasses on the kitchen counter and poured. "I'm one hundred percent sure Briar is on her way to tell Rowena and Sam that she saw you at my place with a very romantic bouquet of flowers."

"I'm glad you liked them." He sipped his wine. "Maybe we just let things follow their natural course."

"And dad? We should definitely tell him the truth."

"Absolutely not." He cocked an eyebrow. "He can't know this is all a ruse. Do you see how that would make me look?"

"Like you don't know what you're doing." I glanced up at him with my glass halfway to my lips. "Sorry. You know what I mean."

"I do, actually. And you're right." He drank some more. "If I knew what I was doing, I wouldn't be taking you out on a date to show everyone that the Christmas spirit is alive and well in Winterstorm Village."

"It sounds awful when you say it like that in your politician voice." As odd as it was being here with Rhett, my gut feeling told me we were doing the right thing. "You get some more liquid courage in you, I'll go get dressed."

"I'll be here." He flashed me a sexy smile that sent a trail of goosebumps up my arm.

I got ready in record time, opting to wear a low-cut sweater, jeans and high boots. I let my hair down and even went a little darker with my eye makeup. A part of me wanted to be at the same level as Rhett. Somehow, the man looked hotter in jeans, more approachable, less the town's Scrooge.

"Cruz." He called from downstairs. "We're losing daylight."

"Oh right. Coming." I rushed out of my bedroom.

When I reached the landing, he stopped to look up at me. We needed ground rules. His whole smoldering thing needed to stop.

"You look nice." He smiled.

"Oh thanks. You too." I met him at the bottom of the stairs.

"You're in charge. What do we do first?" he asked as his gaze met mine.

"Let's stroll around the Arabelle. If there's enough people, we can skate for a little bit and let them see us." I walked past him to grab my purse and heavy coat. "Are you ready?"

"After you." He gestured for me to go on.

I dashed to the front door and swung it open. The minute the frigid air brushed my cheeks, all doubts swirling around in my head vanished. My house was about half a mile from the Arabelle, driving would mean looking for parking, and that would take forever. I turned to tell Rhett, but he beat me to it.

"We should walk." He took me by the hand.

"Yeah, okay." I nodded as I tried really hard not to glance down at our interlaced fingers. "My hands are cold."

"It's fine." He winked.

Not five minutes in, I spotted Sam, Rowena, and Briar. All three of them stood on the corner of Main Street, openly staring at us. How the hell was I going to explain Rhett touching me? They knew I wasn't big on PDA.

Briar gestured toward us as her lips formed the words "I told you." Or something that meant I was up to something with our new mayor.

"Gurl?" Sam mouthed, beaming at me.

Rhett chuckled, then whispered in my ear, "They're put out. But not surprised. How interesting."

"Of course they're surprised. Us together is cosmically wrong. Impossible." I said under my breath so only he could hear me, gently yanking to free my hand. "They're probably worried I fell and hit my head."

"Explain." Rowena braced her hands on her hips as soon as we were within earshot.

"She didn't fall and hit her head, if that's what you're worried about." Rhett kissed the inside of my hand, sending flutters up my arm.

"Is this real?" she asked me.

"Yeah. How about that?" I gave her a sheepish smile. "Enemies to lovers' trope. Um, I mean, no, we're not. Jesus, we're not lovers. It's too soon. You know what I mean."

"No need to be shy, sweetheart." Rhett pulled me closer to his warm body.

"Parker Parker?" Sam asked. "Are you sure, sweetie?"

Jeez, it wasn't like we were running off to get married. It was just a date. A fake date. This was a fake date. I inhaled deeply then quietly released my breath. "We're just seeing where it goes," I said casually, ignoring how perfect my body fit next to Rhett's.

"Parker Parker has a nice ring to it." Rhett tightened his hold around my waist. "Don't you think, Plum Cakes?"

My ears burned hot. "We have reservations at the skating rink," I blurted out. "We don't want to be late."

"You hate skating." Rowena squinted her eyes at Rhett. "Parker told us."

"She did, did she?" He glanced down at me with a knowing smile. He was enjoying this. "Love makes you do crazy things, I guess. Shall we go, Sugar Pie?"

I winced at his term of endearment. He was laying it on thick just for my friends, just to torture me. I was pretty sure this was payback for the one time I paid Frank the city hall janitor twenty bucks to tell Rhett the men's bathroom was out of service. Rhett had to go across the street, which in turn, made him super late to his first meeting with my dad, the mayor. I glanced up at him, past his chiseled jaw and into his playful gaze.

"Yeah." I nodded at him, then turned to my friends. "I'll see you guys later."

"Probably not later." He winked.

Sam, who was sipping from his coffee, started coughing. Oh, they all got his meaning. I elbowed him hard. "We'll text. Bye." I waved goodbye at the trio of stunned faces, while Rhett ushered me down Main Street.

I swore we got away with leaving them without a real explanation because they were too shocked to even ask the right questions. Like, how long have we been dating? Who made the first move? Was he a good kisser?

"Omigod." I shot a quick glance over my shoulder. "That was so embarrassing."

"That would only be embarrassing if you spent a great deal of your time telling your friends how much you hate me. Is that what you do, Sugar Plum? You talk about me when I'm not there?"

"You wish. I rarely think of you." I pulled at my hand, and he let me go. "I need some hot chocolate to calm down."

We stopped at the Chalet Pastry Shop, ordered a couple of peppermint mochas to go, then sat on a bench facing the Arabelle. My chest hurt seeing the old clock tower practically in ruins. The Christmas tree had been set upright again, but the lights were still out. Whatever electrical malfunction happened the night of the storm, they still hadn't fixed it.

"Why don't we get a generator for it?" I sipped from my cup.

"For the Christmas tree?" Rhett sat back and placed his arm on the backrest behind me. "Too loud. And the fumes were bad."

"Right." I shook my head. "I hope they get it fixed soon."

"Why is this holiday such a big deal to you?" he asked, bracing his arms on his knees before he looked at me.

"It was my mom's favorite. Some of my best memories of her happened around Christmas. I don't know. I guess it's a way of keeping her alive." Why the hell did I just say all that? It wasn't like Rhett cared at all. "It's also good for business."

"Right." He stared straight ahead as he drank some more from his cup. After a long moment, he released a breath, then shifted his body to face me. "Why do you hate me?" He pointed behind him, a reference to our little encounter with my friends earlier.

"I don't know. I mean, I don't hate you."

"Then what? During the campaign, it all made sense. But now? We're on the same team, Cruz."

"It's just." I swallowed hard. If we were going to make this work, I had to be honest with him. "You stole my name."

"What?" He furrowed his brows at me.

"Yeah, because of you, I became Parker girl. I hated it." I met his gaze.

"That was in high school. It's been more than ten years."

"It started then. And you're still doing it. I'm not Cruz. I'm Parker." I raised my voice, which made a few people look our way. Crap. This date was not going the way I'd hoped. Erm, fake date.

"I'm sorry. I had no idea." He glanced down at his hand, shaking his head. "I was embarrassed to be back. I didn't think—"

"We should go home," I blurted out.

"You hate me that much?"

"No."

"Then don't chicken out just because your friends didn't like seeing us together." He waved in the general direction of the skating rink. "I'm prepared to go all in. But if you're scared."

"You know I'm not scared." I shot to my feet.

"Then let's go." A sexy smile touched his lips as he took a few steps toward the Arabelle.

I fell into step next to him, as I braced myself for the ultimate date spot in Winterstorm Village. Even though the Christmas tree wasn't lit, a few couples had decided to venture out to hit the ice anyway. For a moment, I stopped to watch them. They all looked so in love. In all the years I've been coming here, I'd never brought a date before. The idea never occurred to me.

"Are you okay?" Rhett stepped into my line of sight.

"Yeah. Why wouldn't I be. Let's do this." Determined to make our plan work, I marched up to the ticket window. "Hi, Jimbo," I greeted the old man working the counter. "You got our tickets?"

"I sure do, Parker." He leaned in to look at Rhett with a knowing smile stretching from ear to ear. He wasn't even surprised to see us together. "Mr. Mayor."

"Jimbo." Rhett dipped his head.

After we got our rental skates on, we headed straight for the ice. I had expected Rhett to be bad at skating. More than once at the office, he'd mentioned skating was a waste of time, same as the Christmas tree lighting ceremony, the Sno-Ball, and even the school play. The man was a real-life Scrooge. Though tonight, he seemed different.

"It's like riding bike." He glided across the ice then came to a perfect stop as he turned to face me.

"Wait. Are you...?" I looked over my shoulder, teasingly. "Are you having fun, Mr. Mayor? I didn't think that was possible."

"Come on." He took my hand and pushed off, taking me with him.

His confident stride made me relax next to him. Bit by bit, the frigid air calmed my nerves, and before I knew it, I had a smile on my face while I skated around the rink next to Rhett. Did the other couples think we looked as happy as them?

I was still flying high, thinking how my genius plan couldn't fail when Sam, Briar, and Rowena appeared in my line of sight on the other side of the square. The sun peeked just above the building tops and painted bright rays on the ice and on their doubtful faces.

Rhett was right. If anyone, not just Dad, found out we were pretending to be in love, Christmas would be ruined. Forever. We couldn't let anyone know the magic wasn't real. We couldn't back down now.

"Rhett." I squeezed his hand and pressed my body to his side. "We have to kiss."

CHAPTER 7

The Olde Windsor Gazette

"I'm sorry what?" Rhett stopped in his tracks as the big Christmas tree loomed over us, casting a gray shadow across the rink.

The look of horror on his face felt like a punch to the stomach. For a minute there, while I was traveling across the ice, practically in his arms, I began to believe we were truly partners in crime. But even if Rhett was being nice to me now, he was still my office nemesis. Something like that couldn't be undone with peppermint mochas and skating.

"Sorry. I'm just panicking. My friends are over there." I pointed behind me.

Rhett peeped at them over my head. "I see them. So?"

"They didn't buy it."

"And you think a kiss is going to sell them on it?" He chuckled. "I thought you said it wouldn't come to this."

"I know what I said." I ran a hand through my hair. "Forget I brought it up. If we stick to our story, we should be fine. In three weeks, the season will be over, and we can go back to hating each other."

"There's that word again." He pulled me to the side to let another couple go by us. "I don't hate you. I never have." With a big sigh, he cocked his head and lifted my chin with his index finger. "If you want to do the kiss thing, I'm game."

"Not if you're repulsed by it." I pressed my hand to his chest.

"I'm not." He shook his head. "And you? Are you repulsed by it?"

I met his serene gaze. The sun had already begun its descent in the horizon, giving way to a twilight bathed in orange and blue hues that seemed to match the blue in his eyes. I'd never noticed his full lips before, how soft they seemed. Once, during the campaign last year, I bumped into him after his and Dad's debate on the town square. Not far from where my friends stood now. I crashed into him so hard, our mouths almost collided. Back then, I was so appalled by it, I shoved him away from me and stomped off. He had also just called me a spoiled brat. So of course I had reason to hate him in the moment.

"Um. I don't think so. I can do it." A shock of adrenaline rushed through me. "Let's see, we should maybe turn this way." I gripped both his arms and shifted his body slightly to the right, so my friends had a better view of us. "Put your hand on my waist." I took his hand in mine. When his eyebrows shot up in surprise, I let him go. "You're right. Now we look like we're at our eighth-grade dance. Um." I braced my palm on his chest. Jeez, the man was solid muscle.

Immediately, images of the day I saw him shirtless in his office flitted through my mind. What the hell was wrong with me? I couldn't think of Rhett like that. He was my boss. This was business.

I removed my hand, and he caught my wrist. "Parker, relax."

My name on his lips unraveled something inside my chest.

He let my fingers rest over his thumping heart. And then, as he cradled my neck, he pressed his soft lips to mine. Snow flurries danced happily around us as a gust of wind rushed across the ice rink. When my eyes fluttered open, bright lights sparked and flew up into the sky.

Fireworks? The man made me see fireworks.

"Hmm." He sighed as he pulled back then whispered, "We should try it with tongue. That'll seal the deal."

I stared up him. My heart pumped so hard, I barely heard myself utter an agreement. "Okay."

More sparks flew overhead, painting the now dark sky with different colors as Rhett bent down again to tease my lips with his. His velvet tongue coaxed mine into a sensual dance that made me melt into him. He tasted of hot chocolate and peppermint and...Christmas.

His body fit mine so perfectly. I had no choice but to let him in as he moved his hand inside my coat and around my waist. I tunneled my fingers through his hair, and he deepened the kiss, holding me tighter as if he were afraid I'd fall if he didn't.

One minute we were plunged into darkness, and then the next, the whole ice rink lit up with bright lights everywhere. I broke the kiss first, laboring to catch my breath. Did he feel it too? I peered into his bright blue eyes. Jesus, what did we just do?

"Did we just fix the Christmas tree lights?" I pointed behind him.

He turned to look just as Jimbo climbed down from the structure holding the entire Christmas tree setup. "The guys finally got it working, Boss." He beamed at Rhett. "What do you think?"

"It looks magical," I mumbled.

"Good work." Rhett waved at Jimbo before he faced me again. "Looks like we're back in business."

"Yeah, we are." I bit my lower lip. "Um, we should call it a day."

"You're right." He made to touch my face, but then stopped. "We've done enough for one evening."

I followed him out of the ice rink. By the time I returned my rental skates and put on my boots, my pulse had slowed down to normal. Though the strange feeling in the pit of my stomach remained. Not as intense as before, but it was still there reminding me of his kiss. Then out of nowhere, the word flashed before my eyes. Desire.

No, no, no. That was not possible. I didn't want Rhett. Sure, he was hot as hell. Lickable as Sam had put it. But that didn't mean I had sexual feelings for him. That was insane—more insane than our fake dating plan.

"Are we going to have to do it again?" His sexy voice filtered through my runaway thoughts.

"What?" I turned to look at him so fast, I lost my balance.

"Whoa." He caught me and pulled me to him all in one fluid motion. "Your friends are still watching us. How many kisses do you think it will take before they believe us." He let out a small laugh.

Was he immune to all this touching and kissing? I was

about to combust, while he stood there with a big smile on his face, completely unfazed, completely unaware that my heart was about to spiral out of my chest.

His warm breath brushed my cheek, and I shivered in his arms. "I need to go home."

"Sure. I'll walk you." He adjusted my coat and buttoned it. "I think we made good progress."

If having the hots for my new boss was progress. Yeah, sure, we'd made plenty of that tonight. "Yeah." I headed toward the clock tower, away from the crowd and my friends.

"They're still watching." He fell into step next to me and took my hand.

Oh, there it was again. White hot adrenaline pulsed through every inch of me. And just because I was a real masochist, I let our kiss play like a movie in my head. How the hell was I supposed to deal with more of that for three whole weeks?

The walk back home felt extra short. Mainly because I didn't want to end our fake date. I was so confused. I wanted Rhett away from me. But also, I couldn't stop wondering what a good-night kiss would be like.

"I would invite you in, but I have to be at work early." I climbed the steps up to my front porch and faced him. "My boss is a real hard ass."

"Is he really that bad?" He closed the space between us with a playful twinkle in his eyes.

"He's a Scrooge." I let out a slow breath.

"Hmm." He leaned in and whispered in my ear, "Good-night, Parker."

I stood there and watched him as he sauntered back to his

car and drove away. Tomorrow was going to be hell in the office.

THE NEXT DAY, I skipped my morning coffee at Rowena's bakery and went straight to work. I wasn't in the mood to answer a million and one questions about Rhett and me. For now, I had to let Rhett's hot kiss do the talking for us. The fact that none of my friends called me last night meant they thought Rhett had spent the night, which was fine by me. The hard part, making the town believe our story, was over. Now I could focus on work and raising funds to keep the holiday festivities on track.

Luckily, a quick glance at Rhett's agenda told me he was in meetings all day. That meant I wouldn't see him at all, which was a good thing because I still wasn't sure why my body had decided we didn't hate Rhett anymore.

"Parker, my office." Rhett's smooth as honey voice boomed over the intercom on my phone.

For no reason at all, my heart skipped a beat. I glared at his door as I tried to calm down. Obviously, the kiss didn't mean much to him last night. If it had, he would've said something. He would've begged me to let him spend the night. At least, that was how the recurring fantasy in my head played out every time I thought of our kiss.

"Parker." He said my name again. This time, I swore there was an undertone to it. As if my name was a secret only the two of us knew about.

"Yeah." I cleared my throat, pushing the intercom button. "Coming." I winced at the breathy tone in my voice. Tossing my pen on the desk, I rose to my feet and headed to his office. I knocked on the door once, then pushed it open to peek my head in the door with my eyes closed. "Are you decent?"

"Yes," he said flatly.

I let myself in and shut the door behind me. "How can I help you, Mr. Mayor?" Crap, why did that sound so kinky? Or was that just me? When I looked up, the look of surprise in his eyes said it all. I was making things weird. "Sorry. I meant..."

"I know what you meant." He gestured to the chair across from him. "We have a bit of a problem."

"Oh yeah." I ambled to his desk but didn't bother to sit. "What happened?"

"The kiss was a mistake."

"Oh." I swallowed the lump in my throat. "Of course it was. I thought so too. I went home feeling a little nauseous." If he had hated it that much, I could too.

"We made the front page on the Olde Windsor Gazette." He showed me the town's local magazine.

"Oh." I reached for it and flipped through the pages until I found the article that went with the picture of us literally making out on the ice. "I mean, the kiss looks real. Good job on that." I shot him a quick glance. I still couldn't get myself to really look at him—not without picturing him shirtless and with his tongue inside my mouth.

I quickly scanned the copy. Basically, the Gazette got it right. *Rhett P. Windsor III and Parker Cruz are officially an item. The happy couple was spotted showing off their Christmas spirit on the ice.*

"This is gold. It couldn't have gone better." I glanced up at Rhett, then it hit me. They'd used his other name. "I'm sorry. Should I call them and get them to print the right name?"

"No, leave it. The damage has already been done." He tossed an envelope with a broken wax seal on his desk. "From Aunt Gretchen. It's for tonight."

"She's still in town?" I took the heavy invitation. I'd always liked Gretchen Windsor. Of all the Windsors, she was the only one who wasn't a pompous ass. Well, her and her brother, Rhett Senior. "Is she having a party?" I glanced down at the letter, and away from Rhett's darkened gaze. He really hated his name.

As I read, I slowly began to understand the kind of trouble we were in. His great-aunt Gretchen wanted to meet her nephew's new girlfriend—me. Oh shit. No, this couldn't be happening. Dinner at the Windsor mansion was meant for royalty and stuff, which I wasn't. Far from it. The Windsors were the co-founders of Winterstorm Village. Sure, I was the mayor's daughter. And technically, now the mayor's girlfriend, but to them, I was no more than a townie.

"This is bad. If she didn't hate me before, she certainly will hate me now. Aren't you supposed to marry some princess from a small country in Europe?"

The babbling wasn't helping. I had been so preoccupied with Christmas, the lack of funding, and Rhett's kiss that I hadn't stopped to think what this would mean for his family and all the plans they had for him.

"It's technically an island. And no, I have no intention of honoring that fucked-up arrangement." He shot to his feet.

"Wait, what? Are you serious? Are you really marrying royalty? I was kidding about that." I placed a hand on my clammy forehead. I'd always assumed the rumors were just that—rumors, a joke because of how high and mighty his whole family acted. Our lie had gone too far. We were meddling in international affairs now. "We should come clean. Like right now."

"We're not doing that. This is bad. But I'm not backing down." He stared at me for the longest time.

"What about your princess?" I slowly set the magazine and invitation on his desk.

"You and I are in love. And that's final." He ran a hand through his hair, then shot me a look of horror. "I mean, as far as the town is concerned, we're in love."

"Of course. The town." I inhaled. "Do you want to talk about it? I mean, every time someone mentions the name Windsor you go all dark."

He faced me with dark murder in his eyes.

"Yep, that's the look." I pointed at his face.

"This is serious, Parker. Are you up to the task, or not? Because convincing my great-aunt that you and I are soul mates is going to take more than a simple kiss."

A simple kiss? Was that what he thought of it? Because to me, that kiss had been soul piercing, magical, the stuff that only happens after a raging snowstorm.

"Parker?"

"Yeah." His voice startled me back to reality. "My dad is still in the hospital recovering. There's a good chance we won't even have to tell him about us—the fake us. My friends already know thanks to your excellent acting skills. But Rhett, if we keep going with this lie, we might ruin your life. Gosh, and this is only day two."

"I know what's at stake, Parker. And trust me, it's more than money or a job."

Our gazes locked, and in an instant, a heated energy killed the chill in the air. I should've thought this through a bit more.

"Why did you agree to my stupid plan if you knew there would be consequences for you?"

"I agreed because this is my town too. I haven't been a Windsor in a very long time. That's not about to change."

"What if she disowns you for this? Is that a thing?"

"She can't disown me if I'm not a Windsor." He took in a breath. "She can't know this is all a ruse. It would make me look like..."

"Like you don't know what you're doing."

"Correct."

Why didn't I see it before? Rhett fought hard every day to do his job as deputy mayor and now mayor because he wanted to build something that was his own. Something his family couldn't touch. I knew something had happened with Rhett's dad a long time ago. But Rhett's family had been gone for so long that no one thought to dig into their scandal or even ask why Rhett came back to town after so many years, not as Rhett Windsor, but as Rhett Parker with no mom or dad.

"What do you want to do?" I asked.

"The only thing we can do. We're going to the dinner party so Aunt Gretchen can meet my official girlfriend."

"Omigod, Rhett." I covered my face with both hands. "I can't do that. Your great-aunt is a nice Windsor, but she can be terrifying. Like a terrifying nana, you know. Like nice, but stern." I was babbling.

"I know." He reached across the desk and took my wrists. When I looked up at him, he continued, "One dinner. That's all I need to prove to her that I'm better off on my own."

CHAPTER 8

I Thought of Christmas

I knocked on Parker's door. At this point, I had grown accustomed to the incessant drumming in my chest. Every time she walked in the room, every time I thought of her, or someone mentioned her, my heart would pick up the pace. Fuck, why did I kiss her? Why did I let my feelings get the best of me?

This whole lie was wrong. But we were now in too deep to back down. The only way to make it through the holidays was to stick to our plan. With a bit of luck, my Windsor problem would be over tonight. Aunt Gretchen was persistent, but at some point, she had to understand I had no interest in being a Windsor ever again. I didn't care about the family fortune or their illustrious name. Many years ago, I learned that those things didn't mean shit.

"Hi." Parker swung the door open, reached for my hand, then pulled me in. "I need your help." She stopped to look at me with her mouth slightly slack. "You're in a tuxedo."

"You're not dressed." My gaze swept down to her bathrobe, then up again. "We can't be late."

"We won't." She shut the door and strode to the living room where she had a whole rack of dresses. "I need help choosing. They're all gorgeous gowns. But I need you to tell me which one is going to knock your great-aunt's socks off into New Year's Eve." She braced her hands on her waist. "I want to make a good impression. For you. I mean, that's the deal, right?"

She was particularly adorable when she rambled on like that. For some reason, she cared to do right by me. I stuffed my hands in the pockets of my tuxedo pants and focused on the task at hand. I had to stop thinking about her pouty lips. Kissing her again would be a huge mistake, bigger than the first time, which was the reason why we were in our current predicament to begin with.

"You don't need to impress anyone. All you have to do is shake a few hands. Tell them we're madly in love and move on." I had a feeling things would be more complicated than that, but for now we had to stick with what we knew.

"I've never been to the Windsor mansion for a private dinner party with not one, but two, founding families. I need them to lose their socks." She furrowed her brows. "You know what I mean."

I reached for her arms and turned her slightly to look me in the eyes. "Don't be nervous. It's just a dinner. And how do you know the Waltons are going to be there?"

"I was freaking out. So, I texted Briar, who texted her bestie Ava. She's the one who sent the dresses over." She pulled two dresses off the rack. "These two are my favorite.

What do you think? I like the sweeping pooled mermaid hem and the off-the-shoulder neckline, but what do you think of the color?" She raised one then the other. "Red vs silver. There's a black one in there too. If red is too much."

Parker would look stunning in any of these dresses. Lately, when I thought of Parker, I thought of Christmas. "The red one."

"Why?"

"I like the embroidery." I made to touch the fabric.

"Don't touch." She yanked the dress out of my reach. "That's an Oscar de La Renta, twelve-grand gown. The floral threadwork embroidered to a sheer effect is very delicate." She stroked it gently. "Yeah, you're right. It's perfect. I don't know what I was thinking before. Turn around."

"Excuse me?"

"I don't have time for modesty. Turn around so I can change here."

I did as she asked, then closed my eyes for good measure. The last thing I needed tonight was to see Parker's tight body without clothes. I didn't need to spend another night wondering what it would be like to touch her soft skin all over.

"Okay, can you zip me up?"

When I faced her, the dress hung from her shoulders while she held it in place at the waist. The zipper went all the way down to the top of her butt. Jesus fuck. Now I had to go all night knowing she wasn't wearing a bra. I did my best to close the zipper without touching her. The warmth of her skin was so alluring. How would she react if I ran my hand up her back and onto the nape of her neck?

Before I could stop it, our kiss played on repeat in my

mind, just like it had done for hours last night. I let out a breath. She did the same as a trail of goosebumps fluttered across her smooth skin.

"Don't move."

"Hmm?" She exhaled.

"I have something for you." I fished a small box from the inside of my tuxedo jacket. "Aunt Gretchen sent me a few things that belonged to my mother when I came back after college. I thought you could wear this tonight." I placed the cold diamond necklace on her chest.

"Omigod. I can't accept this." She strode to the hallway mirror. "Omigod."

"Just for tonight. It goes with your dress."

"Big, chunky diamonds go with everything." She turned to meet my gaze. "What am I getting into tonight, Rhett? Is your great-aunt going to offer me money to give you up?" She beamed at me as she ambled to the kitchen counter to grab a piece of paper. "Because I made a list. The repairs on the library roof can't wait. And don't get me started on the clock tower. It's going to cost a fortune to repair it. Last we checked, including donations, we only have five thousand dollars."

"Of course you made a list." I shook my head. "Negotiate away. Here's a tip. Aunt Gretchen is desperate. She'll pay big to see me free of you."

"Thank you." She slapped my chest playfully. "What happens when I'm out of the picture? What does she want from you?"

"Don't worry about that." I wrapped my fingers around her wrist and kissed the inside of it before I realized what I was doing. "We should go before Aunt Gretchen's checkbook gets cold. Is this you?" I pointed at the black coat lying on the back of the sofa, ignoring her confounded look.

"Yes. Thank you." She tiptoed to the couch and slipped on a pair of slingbacks, giving me an ample display of her cleavage in the process.

This was a terrible idea. Why did I let her talk me into this crazy plan? Right. Because as much as I like fighting with Parker, I couldn't say no to her. Not when it mattered. Not after all this time.

"Okay. I think I have everything." She reached for a small purse, then turned around so I could drape the long heavy coat over her shoulders. "Thanks." She met my gaze.

For the first time ever, there was no contempt in her eyes. The girl who loved everyone but me didn't seem to hate me anymore. I wished I'd thought to call for a cease-fire years ago.

"Don't thank me yet. After tonight, you might hate me a little more." I winked at her.

"I don't hate you, Rhett." She smiled, shaking her head. "Let's go. You're making us late."

"Me?" I ushered her toward the front door. "You were literally in your bathrobe ten minutes ago."

"Shh." Parker stopped halfway down the stoop to look at me. "A stretch limo?"

"I think Aunt Gretchen was afraid we'd change our minds." I leaned in and caught the scent of her sweet perfume. "You can still bail if you want."

"Never." She dug her index finger into my chest. "I'm not a chicken. And you know it."

I chuckled as I gestured for our driver to stay put so I could be the one to help her inside the limo.

The Windsor mansion was twenty minutes outside of

Winterstorm Village, nestled in the foothills. I had not visited that place since I graduated college. Back then, Grandad was still alive. We fought constantly about the kind of man he wanted me to be. I had no idea who I wanted to be, only that I didn't want to be like Dad—the man who married an artist full of dreams, only to crush her spirit a few years later.

"What would your mom say if she knew you were letting your fa..." She shot a quick glance to the limo driver, then corrected, "Your girlfriend parade around with her jewelry?"

"She would say keep it. She never cared for that stuff." I paused to look at her. I wanted her to know the truth, but did she even care? "It's why she moved to California and changed our last name."

"Oh." She shifted her body to face me. "I guess I knew that. You left before fifth grade started. When you came back junior year, you were no longer Rhett Windsor the third."

I chuckled. "Mom still hates that name."

"Wait. What?" She reached for my hand. "Your mom is alive?"

"Of course she's alive. Why would you think she isn't?" I scoffed. "I supposed the family needed everyone to think she was dead. My parents' marriage and later their divorce was a bit of a scandal within their circle. Now you understand what we're dealing with."

"That's heavy." Parker took in a deep breath. "Then, why are we here? If you don't care about being disowned, and neither does your mom."

"Aunt Gretchen is important to me. I don't want to be part of the family because they always treated my mother like an outsider. But Aunt Gretchen is like a grandmother to me. She was there for me when Granddad made me come back."

"I'm sorry." She placed a hand over her mouth. "I didn't know that."

"Mr. Windsor." The driver met my gaze in the rearview mirror. "We're here."

I opened my mouth to tell him I wasn't a Windsor, but what would be the point? He was here to get paid, not deal with my family crap. "Thank you." I nodded and waited for him to pull up to the front of the house.

One of the ushers opened the door for us. I climbed out of the car, then offered Parker my hand. She took it without even looking at me. Her attention was set on the mansion's facade and all the twinkling Christmas lights.

"Omigod." Her cheeks turned a pretty pink. "There's a good chance I'm in way over my head here."

We both were.

"You'll be fine." I wrapped my arm around her waist and pulled her closer to me. "Just don't leave my side."

Inside, Aunt Gretchen's butler met us in the foyer. "Rhett, it's good to see you."

"Good to see you too. Mark, let me introduce you to Ms. Parker Cruz." My chest tightened when I considered my next words. "My girlfriend."

"Nice to meet you." A pale Parker offered Mark her hand.

Now that I had said the words aloud, there was no going back. For better or worse, Parker Cruz was my girlfriend. "Before you throw us to the wolves, Mark, care to give us a quick rundown of the guest list."

"Of course." He nodded once. "The Walton family is all here, including their children, Ava and Thoren."

"Thor is here?" I winced. "Oh fuck. Okay."

He went on to list forty other families, none of whom lived

in town. They all had flown in from the city to attend my great-aunt's dinner party. They were here to support her in whatever plans she had for Parker and me tonight. Truth was, Parker wasn't that far off the mark. Before the night was over, I was one thousand percent sure Aunt Gretchen would try to buy her out. No doubt she had my best friend Thor on standby to draw up the paperwork.

"Enjoy the party." Mark gestured for us to go on in.

"How about a dance?" I asked Parker.

For one, I didn't feel like making introductions just yet. But also, I was dying to feel Parker's body in my arms again. Especially now that we were in public, and she felt compelled to run her hands all over me—to sell our story. To her, this whole charade was a strategic game. I knew that. My body not so much.

"This place is incredible." She pointed at the row of Christmas trees lining the main hallway.

"Wait 'til you see the ballroom." I leaned in closer.

"Of course there's a ballroom." She gripped the sleeve of my tuxedo jacket tighter.

"Relax, Parker," I whispered in her ear as I ushered her past the heavy double doors. "I won't let anyone hurt you."

"I believe you." She offered me a kind smile, one I'd only seen her bestow on her dad. "You guys call this an intimate dinner? This is a shindig."

I chuckled.

Growing up, Grandad used to throw these lavish Christmas parties. They were one of the few things Mom and I enjoyed together—maybe because it was the only time we felt like we belonged. We used to sneak into the ballroom to help decorate the Christmas trees. Every year, the theme was the same. Every year, the ballroom was draped in garlands, lights, and heavy silks until it felt like we were walking into Charles Dickens' novel, *A Christmas Carol.*

"I've died and gone to heaven." Parker beamed at me. "Is this place real?"

"I'm afraid so."

"If it isn't the happy couple." Thor Walton patted me hard on the back with the biggest smile on his face.

"Parker, you remember Thor." I gestured in his direction.

"Sure. Hi, Thor."

"I'm glad you could make it." He took the hand she offered him and kissed it.

Thor and I had been friends since we were kids. We kept in touch even during my California stint. But the truth was, he couldn't be trusted around women. Mainly because women seemed to lose their minds around him. All he had to do was smile at them—like he was doing now.

"That's enough." I gently shoved him away from her. "Maybe we need a drink before that dance, huh?" I asked Parker as I flagged down a server carrying a tray of champagne flutes.

"Excellent idea." She accepted the champagne, while she admired the Christmas carolers who, true to the party's theme, were dressed in nineteenth century frock.

"Could we talk?" Thor leaned in. "Five minutes."

"Not tonight, Thor. Aunt Gretchen promised to give the family business a rest for a while." I shot a quick glance at Parker.

"Two minutes. You don't want to go into tonight blindly." He gave me a meaningful look.

"Fine." The last thing I wanted to do was leave Parker

alone. I wasn't ready to tell him the truth about the nature of my relationship with Parker, but he needed to know that I had not changed my mind about Aunt Gretchen's proposal. "But I'm going to need something stronger than champagne."

"Ava." Thor whisper-shouted to his little sister, then waved her over. "Do you mind?" He dipped his head toward Parker.

"Hi, Rhett." Ava kissed my cheek. "You look dapper."

"Thank you." I wrapped my arm around Parker's waist.

Parker looked up at me in surprise, as if she didn't remember we were supposed to be in love. "Oh. Ava, hi." She beamed at Ava and hugged her. "I owe you big time. The dresses you sent are gorgeous."

"You're rocking this number." Ava eyed Parker's dress appreciatively. "I'm glad I could help. And I'm so glad you're here. These things can be so boring. Now that you two are here, I know it'll be the party of the season."

"Why don't you two ladies chat for a bit?" Thor cut in. "I need to steal Rhett for two minutes." He grabbed my arm and pulled me toward the bar.

"Sorry." I mouthed to Parker.

Jesus, two days ago I was a free man, living life on my own terms. Now I was here apologizing to Parker for leaving her to talk to my friend. What the hell have I done? I needed to tell Thor the truth before this got out of hand—more than it already had. This was only our second date, and Parker was already meeting Aunt Gretchen and her Upper East Side friends. At this rate, if we weren't careful, Parker and I would be tying the knot before the end of the holiday season.

"Two whiskeys, please." Thor leaned on the bar. "Make them doubles."

"So, what's so important you had to drag me away from my

girlfriend." I took the tumbler he offered, then stopped. Those words were starting to sound way too comfortable.

"I told you the clock was ticking." He exhaled as he scanned the room. "Sofia is here."

"Why is she here?" I rubbed the side of my face.

"Why do you think? She's here for you. Maybe bringing Parker here tonight wasn't such a good idea."

CHAPTER 9

What's Your Number?

Parker

"You and Rhett, huh? That's amazing. I'm so happy for you." Ava chinked my champagne flute. "I was still reading the article in the Olde Windsor Gazette when Briar texted."

"It's a little crazy, I know." I sipped from my glass.

"Honestly, I was hoping Rhett would find someone soon. Maybe now he won't hate Christmas so much. After all the stuff that happened with his dad." She waved her hand in dismissal. "This is a good thing."

"What happened with his dad?" I asked.

"Ms. Cruz?" Mark, the butler, appeared out of nowhere to hand me an envelope.

I opened it and took out a handwritten note signed by Gretchen Windsor herself. She was so old school. Why not send a text?

"I can escort you." Mark smiled politely.

"Well there it is." Ava peeked at the note. "You've been summoned."

"I need to find Rhett." I scanned the room, but didn't see him. Had he left? Someone his size was hard to miss even in a crowded room. "I can't just leave."

"I'll tell him." Ava met my gaze. "Don't make her wait."

"Right. Thank you." I patted Ava's arm before I turned to Mark. "Lead the way."

I followed Mark down the main hallway, across an expansive living room, until he reached a set of double doors. He pushed them open to reveal a library lined with bookcases on all sides. Like the rest of the mansion, this room was also decorated for Christmas with three Christmas trees to the right and fresh garlands hanging from the ceiling.

"This place is a dream."

"Ms. Windsor loves the holidays." He gestured toward the massive desk and chairs at the far end of the room. "She will be with you shortly."

"Thanks." I strolled inside and headed straight for the crackling fire.

What'd happened with Rhett's dad to make him hate Christmas? Rhett had obviously grown up with plenty of holiday cheer. A part of me wanted to apologize to him for all the times I called him a Scrooge. Not once did I stop to think that maybe he had good reason to want to fly off to some beach where Christmas wasn't such a big deal.

I brought my hand up to the diamond necklace he let me borrow. Of course, he'd done it to show his great-aunt that he loved me, that I was part of his life now. But the hopeless romantic in me loved the gesture, even if it wasn't real. I braced both hands on the backrest of a club leather chair. Every time I thought of him as mine, my legs turned to jelly. He wasn't for me. Jesus Christ, he was literally supposed to marry royalty.

Did Gretchen Windsor have a particular princess in mind? Or was she planning to put Rhett on the auction block? Was that even a thing?

"Oh, I'm sorry. I didn't realize this room was occupied." A woman about my age in a stunning sapphire blue dress leaned against the closed door. "Do you mind if I stay a bit? I'm hiding from my bodyguard."

"Stay as long as you want." I ambled toward her and offered her my hand. "I'm Parker Cruz."

"Yes, I know. You made quite an entrance." She shook my hand.

"I did?"

"You're rocking that dress. And, oh that Harry Winston." She beamed at me then shifted her gaze to ogle the necklace properly. "I've only seen it in pictures. I'm Sofia, by the way."

"Nice to meet you." I pointed at the door. "Should I check to see if the coast is clear?"

"Yes, please. I think the upstairs bedrooms might be a better hiding place." She stepped aside to make room for me.

"So what's his deal, your bodyguard? Is he like an evil stepdad or something?" Slowly, I opened the door and peeked outside. When I didn't see anyone, I let the door swing open.

"No, he's just new. And grumpy. And thinks I'm made of glass." She blew out a breath. "I just needed a few moments away from him."

"There's no one out there." I peeked outside again. "Maybe he got the hint."

"Maybe. Thanks for the help." She sounded a bit disappointed as she headed out. "It was nice meeting you." She waved goodbye as she slowed down halfway up the grand staircase.

"Likewise." I called after her and watched as the hem of her dress disappeared as soon as she reached the landing.

"I can see why he likes you."

"Hmm?" I did a double take when I saw Gretchen Windsor, the only surviving sister of the late Rhett Windsor Senior, the matriarch of the Windsor family, and Rhett's second grandmother. "Hello, Ms. Windsor. I'm Parker Cruz." I bit my tongue before I followed my name with *the mayor's daughter*. A part of me wanted to add titles to my name.

"I know who you are, dear." She gestured toward the library.

Right, whatever she had to say to me had to be said in private. She might even make me sign a non-disclosure agreement. I was prepared to do all that. The town needed the Windsor money. I was not above begging for donations. That was literally my job.

I ambled inside and headed straight for the roaring fire again. Somehow the fireplace felt like neutral territory compared to the massive wooden desk with the giant floor-to-ceiling windows as the backdrop. At night, everything looked darker beyond the glass. But I knew enough of the mansion to know there was a beautiful garden surrounding the property.

"You met Sofia." Gretchen strode to her desk in her elegant black gown with sequins embroidered in a delicate pattern. The woman oozed old money and power. A part of me desperately wanted to be her friend. The other part of me was too terrified to even look her in the eyes. "You truly are a magnet for trouble."

"Trouble does tend to find me." I thought it best not to mention that her great-nephew was the biggest trouble to ever find me.

"I appreciate your honesty." She sat, pulled out the latest issue of the Olde Windsor Gazette and tossed it on the desk. "You seem to have made an impression on Rhett."

I stepped closer to look just to confirm we were on the same page. Wow, that kiss looked so hot. What? No. I had to focus and not think about how it felt to be kissed like that.

"We were swept away by the magic of the season." I played my only card. Winterstorm Village was known for its romance. Wasn't that why I was in this bloody mess? Okay, so technically the mess had not gotten bloody yet, but based on Gretchen's shrewd face, we were about to get there. "With all that's happened, the townspeople appreciated some happy news."

I stopped talking while Gretchen did the math. Or maybe she was pretending to assess me just to throw me off. We both knew she was here to offer me money. We also knew, she'd done her homework on me. I had to assume she knew all my dirty secrets. Did she know about my rivalry with Rhett? Did it matter to her that I was president of the chess club when I was in high school? Somehow, of all the things I'd achieved in life, that was the only accolade that seemed to fit our current situation.

Unlike Rhett's striking good looks, Gretchen had more of an understated beauty. She seemed ageless. "How much do you think it would take to give them a different kind of happy news? The townspeople," she added.

"We're always grateful for your family's donations." I smiled.

"How grateful?" she asked.

At twenty-eight, I couldn't be considered a seasoned politician. If this was one-hundred percent business, I could keep this level of bullshit going. But in the past couple of days, I'd gotten to know Rhett a bit more. I was curious to learn more. If I was going to sell us all out, I wanted Gretchen to spell it out.

"We all have our number, Ms. Windsor. For example, my number is two. Two million dollars to complete the repairs the local library needs, the school needs more books, and don't get me started on the clock tower." I met her gaze. "What's your number, Ms. Windsor?"

No idea why I asked that.

Her eyes shot up in surprise. "My number?" She exhaled and sat back as if giving my question careful consideration. "My number is one. One viable heir. One empire, one empty seat. Rhett is all I have left."

I thought of the guest list Mark recounted when Rhett and I arrived earlier. At least, three of those families were closely related to the Windsors, and four others were actual Windsors. "You seem to have a whole roomful of heirs in there." I pointed in the general direction of the ballroom.

She scoffed. "They're all useless. Birds for brains. They could never take over the family's media conglomerate. Not like Rhett."

"They have CEOs for that, don't they?" I was really stepping out of line. What the hell was I doing? She hadn't even flinched when I asked for two million dollars. So what was my deal? "You don't need Rhett."

Stop talking, Cruz. Erm, Parker.

"He has a duty to uphold. He likes to pretend he doesn't, but he knows better than that." She pointed at our hot kiss printed in full color. "He knows better than this. He's my brother's direct descendant."

"What are you offering me?"

"I appreciate your candor, Ms. Cruz. I'll be honest too. This home belongs to Rhett. Soon he'll need to be ready. A wife and a title are waiting for him. I was hoping he would be finished with the town by now. I'm running out of time." She paused for several breaths. "There are worse things than being a Duke's mistress."

Jesus, I'd gone from fake girlfriend to Duke's mistress in two dates flat. If this were a historical romance, I might jump on the opportunity. But we were talking about Rhett's very real life here. If he truly wanted this mansion and a princess for a wife, he would've skipped the grueling year-long campaign to become mayor and moved to the city instead. He would've chosen a princess, instead of a fake date with me.

"Set him free. Convince him to accept his grandfather's legacy, to sit at the head of the table like he was supposed to do three years ago, and I will personally ensure you get a brand-new library, a school, and a clock tower. I'll even make sure your father gets re-elected when the time comes."

That was easily more than the two million dollars I had asked for.

"That's a very nice offer. And I truly understand why you're doing it. If I had the ability to do what you want me to do, to convince Rhett of anything, I would gladly help. But here's the thing." I stopped to inhale. Suddenly there wasn't enough air in the room, and my chest hurt. "The thing is, Rhett isn't mine to give up. I can't make him do all the things you just said."

Truly, I didn't have that kind of pull with him. But also, Rhett would never be happy marrying some princess. He belonged in Winterstorm Village. Why did I even care if Rhett married someone else, or had babies? Babies? Jesus. Did she say babies or was that all me?

"And there's your answer, Aunt Gretchen."

I spun around to find Rhett casually leaning on the doorframe. How long had he been there? I opened my mouth to explain to him why I couldn't accept his great-aunt's money, but I couldn't come up with the right words, especially when he was looking at me with so much pain in his eyes.

"That appears to be the case." She sat back in her chair. "Did you speak with Thor?"

"I did." Rhett nodded. "My answer hasn't changed. I'm the mayor now. I can't just pick up and leave."

"A waste of your talents." Gretchen rolled her eyes as she grabbed the magazine and stuffed it back in the desk drawer.

"Parker, let's go. I want to show you something." Rhett offered me his hand.

Without thinking, I reached for it and held it tight. I wanted to tell him he wasn't alone. I was here for him, along with the rest of the town.

"Enjoy the party." Gretchen smiled at us.

Rhett escorted me out of the library and shut the door behind him. Out in the main hallway, Mark greeted us with both our coats hanging over his arm.

"Are we leaving?" I asked Rhett.

"No, we're just going for a walk." He winked at me.

I let him drape my coat over my shoulders, then waited while he donned his own. The far end of the living room, like the library, had a view of the gardens. To my surprise, that was exactly where we were headed. Mark rushed in front of us and opened the double doors.

The frigid air filled my lungs and put a smile on my face

again. Of course, the outside was also decked out with lights, shiny ornaments, and garland. Christmas tunes played over the speakers as we strolled down the gravel path, away from the house.

"If you were my real girlfriend, I'd be so pissed off right now," he said through gritted teeth.

"You're not?" I glanced at him. He was definitely fuming. I pressed my forehead to his shoulder. "I couldn't accept the money. It felt wrong."

"We'll find another way to pay for your precious clock."

"It's a symbol of our community and how far we've come—"

"I know what the clock tower is to this town, Parker."

I blew out a breath. "We'll get the money some other way. Maybe not in time for Christmas. But we'll get there."

"Well, for what it's worth, thank you for not selling me out." He flashed me a sexy smile.

"My pleasure." I laughed, then did a double take. "What is that?"

"The thing I wanted to show you."

"Omigod. Is that a replica of the Olde Windsor?" I darted toward the clock tower to get a better look.

"Yes and no. It's a similar design, built a few decades after the clock tower that was installed in the town square." He stood next to me, also looking up. "The one in town used to be right here. Until my great-great-grandmother decided it was too old and dingy to sit in the middle of these beautiful gardens. She had a new one made and donated the existing one to the town. Hence the name, the Olde Windsor. This is the new one." He chuckled.

"It's gorgeous." I smiled at it. "Wait. Is that a mistletoe at the top?"

"Where?" He followed my line of sight ten feet up. "I guess it is." His gaze swept down to my profile.

In an instant, the air around us shifted, and my whole body reacted. Since when was this a thing between us? Why did I feel all warm inside every time I thought about our kiss? Rhett wasn't mine. He couldn't be. His great-aunt was very clear on that matter. And just because he didn't want to be their pet, didn't mean he wanted to be with me.

Our arrangement was purely business.

"Aunt Gretchen is looking this way." He stepped closer and cupped my cheek. His smolder was unbearable. "Don't look. Let her think we're so in love we're oblivious to anything around us," he whispered as his gaze shifted from mine down to my lips then up again.

Even if I had wanted to turn around and see for myself, I didn't think I could. Rhett's intense gaze could be so hypnotic. And more than that, I didn't dare move because I wanted him to kiss me again. I couldn't deny that anymore.

"Okay," I mumbled.

"If we don't kiss..." He let the consequences linger in the air.

"She'll know the truth."

"We don't want that." He wrapped his arm around my waist and held me closer. "Do we?"

"No." I bit my lip. "It would be a disaster."

Desire pulsed through me. I recognized it for what it was now. And I didn't even care that Rhett didn't feel the same way. I wanted to feel his mouth on me again. Before he changed his mind on how far he was willing to take our devious plan, I slid my hand up his hard chest and into his hair.

With a sigh of surrender, he bent down and pressed his mouth to mine. He kissed me twice like that before he ran the tip of his tongue across the seam of my lips. I parted them slightly, and he did the rest, deepening our connection, igniting something inside me I'd never felt before.

I should tell him we were playing with fire, that I was wrong in thinking I could get this close to him and not be affected by him, that if we continued down this path there would be no going back for me. But then he'd pull away. And I didn't want him to do that.

His long fingers found the nape of my neck as he continued to claim my mouth in a heated kiss. My chest rose and fell while I labored to catch my breath and contain what I now knew to be want and lust.

I was officially fake, fake dating my grumpy boss.

CHAPTER 10

There's Always a Choice

Parker

"You have to stop kissing me like this," I whispered on his lips.

"This is the only way I know how," he muttered, capturing my mouth once more. After what felt like no time at all, he lifted his gaze toward the library window. "She's gone." He cleared his throat. "We should head back inside."

"Yeah." I took a single step away from him, doing my best to pretend his kiss hadn't seared right through my soul. "Let's um..." I swallowed. "Let's try and stay away from mistletoe going forward."

"Good idea." He smiled at me.

The seemingly innocuous gesture put all kinds of bad ideas in my head. In an instant, I saw Rhett shirtless in his office again, then for no reason at all, I saw him in my room, kissing me, and...

"We'll make an excuse after dinner and go home." He interrupted my impromptu fantasy.

"Great plan, Boss." I said in a too bubbly tone.

"Boss?" He chuckled, furrowing his brows. After a beat, he reached for my hand. "Parker—"

"Rhett!" A woman called out from the house.

I turned to find Sofia at the top of the garden path, waving enthusiastically. "Gretchen told me I'd find you out here." She rushed toward him and planted a big kiss on his cheek. She took in a deep breath and beamed at him. She had one of those blinding smiles. I swore I saw tiny red hearts float around her then pop when they reached Rhett. "It's so good to see you." A handful of seconds later, she turned to me. "Hi again, friend."

"Hi." I waved, suddenly feeling like a third wheel even though she was the one barging in on our date. Erm. Fake date.

"You two know each other?" Rhett stepped back.

"Yeah, we met earlier in the library." My gaze shifted from Rhett to Sofia then back to Rhett.

"We did." Sofia closed the space between her and Rhett and wrapped her arm around his, effectively flushing her entire body against him. She offered me the sweetest smile. "I'm always happy to meet Rhett's friends."

Wait, what? I met Rhett's gaze. I got the sense that I was missing a big clue. "What's going on?" I zeroed in on the swell of her breasts rubbing all over my fake boyfriend.

"Oh, I'm sorry." Sofia placed a hand over her heart as if she was truly sorry. "I'm Rhett's fiancée. Did Gretchen not tell you?"

"Sofia." Rhett peeled her hand off his chest.

"Oh, right." She simultaneously took a step back and pushed Rhett toward me. "It's an arranged marriage. We're not really together, together. I know you're here as his date. It's all good. I don't mind." She met his gaze.

The pink cheeks and desolate look in her eyes told me she totally did mind. More than that, she seemed to be in love with Rhett. Who could blame her? I'd been fake dating Rhett for all of two days, and I was already feeling things that were one hundred percent not part of our agreement. Life was so much easier when Rhett acted like a Scrooge.

"We should go inside." Rhett cleared his throat. "Dinner is probably being served right about now."

"Of course." Sofia looked at him expectantly.

"I'm sorry." Rhett mouthed to me.

Technically, he should escort his fiancée inside. But I was here as his date. Sofia didn't know about our arrangement. And while Rhett wasn't mine to keep, I wasn't about to let Sofia treat me like a third wheel. I didn't care if she was a princess or a duchess, or whatever she was.

"You ready, babe?" I snaked my arm around Rhett's waist, and then, rubbed my breasts against his side for good measure.

"Babe?" he whispered in my ear.

"Oh right." Sofia's eyes watered. She blinked quickly then plastered on a smile. "I'll see you two inside." She waved and scurried toward the house.

As soon as she was out of sight, I let go of Rhett. To my surprise, he caught my hand and brought me closer to him. "I'm sorry. Thor told me she was here. I came to find you to explain but then..." He gestured toward his aunt's library and then the clock as a reference to all the things that had gotten in the way since he found me.

"But then, we got distracted."

"Exactly."

"And you were pissed off at your aunt."

"Yeah." He released a breath.

"Relax, Rhett." I patted his chest. "You don't owe me an explanation. We're fake dating, remember?"

"I remember." He met my gaze. "I still don't want you to feel like..."

"A third wheel?"

"Jesus." He ran a hand through his hair. "Let me explain."

"Nope. We're not together, together, Rhett. So no. You don't need to explain anything to me." I offered him a smile. "We stick to the plan. Dinner. Then home. Once we save Christmas, we can go back to our old lives. And everyone lives happily ever after. Simple."

"Yes. Simple." He glanced away for a beat before he offered me his hand. "You ready, Plum Cake?"

"It's Sugarplum. Get your fairies straight." I winked at him.

Never in a million years would I have thought that fake dating Rhett would be as easy as this. I glanced down at our intertwined hands as we crossed the threshold into the living room. After our encounter with Sofia, the fiancée, Rhett seemed more at ease. As much as he said he hated being a Windsor, he seemed at home here. If I didn't know about all the strings that came with being in this mansion and being Rhett P. Windsor III, I'd say Rhett was truly happy here.

"Dinner is served, Rhett." Mark met us inside to take our coats. "I'll show you to your seats."

"Lead the way." Rhett motioned for Mark to go ahead then pulled me closer to him.

He was so good at selling the whole boyfriend-slash-girlfriend farce. I fell into step next to him and let the fantasy of the date take over. Who wouldn't want to go out with a Windsor? I wasn't that clueless. Half the town was in love with

Rhett and his patrician jawline. I'd seen Mrs. Birdwhistle and her book club ogling him on more than one occasion. And Sam? Sam was a lost cause.

Mark ushered us through the ballroom to the side double doors on the far left, past the bar. When he pushed the doors open, my breath hitched. The long table, which was big enough to seat at least fifty people was decorated with elaborate tall centerpieces, candles, and fruit. I had a clear vision of the ghost from Christmas present sitting among the superfluity. His dinner table would look exactly like this one.

"Your family really likes *A Christmas Carol*," I whispered to Rhett.

"There are three dining rooms like this one around the ballroom." He cocked an eyebrow.

"Let me guess, one for each ghost. Brilliant." I beamed at him.

"Enjoy." Mark pulled a chair out for me.

"Thank you." I sat, relieved to see Ava sitting on my left and Rhett to my right.

"Hi neighbor." Ava gave me a half-hug. "I heard you met Sofia the First."

"The Disney princess?" I asked before I realized she was talking about Princess Sofia.

"The fiancée." She pointed to the other side of Rhett.

"Oh." I sipped from the champagne flute in front of me. "We met. She's lovely."

I tried not to dwell on the fact that Rhett was sandwiched between his arranged fiancée and his fake girlfriend. This night couldn't get any weirder for me. If I were dating Rhett for real, I'd be offended by this setup. But the truth was, Rhett wasn't mine. And my ego had no reason to have opinions on anything. I had to stay focused and not lose sight of the fact that the only reason Rhett and I were at the Windsor mansion pretending to be in love was because Winterstorm Village needed magic.

"She is." Ava rolled her eyes. "It's hard to hate her. But I'm shipping you two so hard." She pointed at Rhett then me.

"Really?" I shot a quick glance at Rhett, who was now in deep conversation with Sofia the First.

"The whole town is. It's too bad the contract can't be undone. Well, you know, without the Windsor family going bankrupt." Ava sipped from her glass, then waved at the couple across from her.

"But Rhett never agreed to that."

"From what my brother has said, there's a contract." She patted my hand with her eyes full of pity. "He has no choice."

"There's always a choice." I sat back to let the server place an amuse-bouche in front of me.

"Smoked salmon macaron with edible gold." He gestured toward the tiny morsel on my plate. "Dill sauce and beluga caviar. Enjoy."

"How many of these courses do we have?" I leaned toward Rhett and placed my hand on his thigh to get his attention.

Rhett glanced up for a breath before he took my hand in his to kiss it. "Twelve." He met my gaze. "We're here for a while. I'm sorry."

"No worries at all. I'm loving this. I could use more gold in my diet, you know." I shrugged, smiling.

"Thank you." He squeezed my hand then let it go.

"This is delicious." Sofia placed her hand on his thigh but quickly retrieved it when she realized Rhett was talking to me now.

I used my left hand to pick up the macaron and popped it in my mouth. The bite was an explosion of flavor in my mouth. It was incredible. "Wow, it really is." I placed my hand on Rhett's thigh again, this time going a little higher. "You should try it, babe."

Who would've thought I was the possessive type? As nice as Sofia was as a person, I still didn't like her pawing my boyfriend...fake boyfriend.

"What are you doing?" Rhett squeezed my fingers gently as he leaned in and whispered in my ear.

"What?" I glanced down at our hands, then up into his mesmerizing blue eyes. "Nothing."

"Parker..." He nuzzled my neck and let my name linger in the air as if he had something else to say.

"Hmm?" I leaned in.

Adrenaline rushed through me the way it had done the night we kissed on the ice rink. For a moment, I didn't care that we were at a Christmas dinner with a roomful of mostly strangers. I rubbed his thigh again since that was the only part of him I had access to. In the distance, a woman cleared her throat. When I glanced up, I met Gretchen's cold stare at the head of the table, three seats down. She didn't seem mad, but she wasn't pleased either.

"Cauliflower puree on a pesto tart, topped with edible flowers and carrot shavings." The server to my right placed a dish in front of me. "Enjoy, Ms. Cruz."

"Thank you." I fixed the napkin on my lap before turning to face Rhett.

"Enjoy your flowers." He winked.

"My favorite." I laughed.

He did too, and something unraveled in my chest. And just

because my brain really liked to torture me, I pictured him shirtless again. But this time, I skipped the office scene and went straight to my bedroom. To my surprise, he didn't seem out of place standing in the middle of all my things, smoldering at me.

"I trust our mayor is doing better." Gretchen burst my fantasy bubble as she calmly sipped from her glass. "When can we expect him back in city hall."

"He is doing much better. He's making a miraculous recovery." I stopped to glance across the table from me. Suddenly all eyes were on me. "He should be home in a couple of weeks."

"I'm happy to hear that." She smiled politely before switching her attention to Rhett. "I need my great grand-nephew in New York."

"I'm happy to advise on whatever you need." Rhett took my hand and placed it on his lap.

"You know what I really need, Rhett." She picked up her spoon and started working on the next course, a small silver bowl filled with broth and two duck dumplings.

"This broth is delicious, Gretchen." Sofia said. "My compliments to the chef."

"Thank you, dear. I will let him know." She glanced over her shoulder. When Mark leaned in, she whispered something to him. I could only assume she was asking him to relay Sofia's message.

By the time I finished my broth, the tension in the air had dissolved and everyone had returned to their conversations. To my left, Ava was telling a story from when her and Thor were little and were forced to sit through their first Christmas dinner at Windsor mansion. I'd known Ava since we were kids because her brother Thor was in my grade. But I'd never really talked to her. She was hilarious and down to earth—the complete opposite of her grumpy, obnoxiously pompous (Briar's words not mine) brother.

"I promise that was the worst of it," Rhett whispered in my ear.

"She's so intense."

"You're doing great." He touched my cheek with the back of his fingers. "Thank you."

In all the years I'd known Rhett, he'd never had an official girlfriend. The day I called him a playboy billionaire acting the politician was because he showed up to the townhall debate with a supermodel from the city. I was offended on behalf of the town, and I let him know it. But now sitting here with Sofia and Gretchen, I understood why he couldn't date like a normal person. His aunt was never going to let him have true love.

"My pleasure. What are fake girlfriends for?" I said so only he could hear me.

As Rhett promised, the rest of the eight courses came and went uneventfully. And after several glasses of wine, Gretchen let loose a tiny bit and even told stories of her late brother and baby Rhett that were actually quite funny.

"You're staying right?" Ava tapped my shoulder to get my attention. "It's tradition. The brunch is my favorite part. You don't want to miss it."

"Oh, I wasn't planning on staying. I didn't pack an overnight bag."

"Nonsense. Of course, you're staying." Gretchen sat regally in her chair. "I will not take no for an answer."

"That means she'll be offended if you don't stay." Sofia chimed in. "You two have to stay. The brunch is to die for."

"I insist," Gretchen added, then leaned back to get her

butler's attention. "Mark, make sure there's a room ready for Ms. Cruz. And whatever else she'll need."

"Right away, ma'am." Mark rushed out of the dining hall.

"I guess I'm staying." I drank from my glass.

"Yay." Ava chinked my empty glass. "And now you don't have to worry about driving in this weather. It's nasty out there."

So much for eating dinner, heading home, and saving Christmas. I glanced over at Rhett who, to my surprise, looked absolutely terrified. We'd never spent a night under the same roof. Technically, this mansion had many roofs—twenty bedrooms, three dining rooms, a library.

I was already spending many hours of my day in the same building as him. Spending the night meant nothing. Or rather, it changed nothing about our agreement and our fake relationship. Come Christmas, Rhett and I had to be done so he could marry a princess.

CHAPTER 11

I Look Like Ebenezer Scrooge

Parker

Three hours later, after dinner ended with two dessert courses and a homemade aperitif, I was more than ready for bed. Ava and her friends returned to the ballroom bar for another round of drinks. I was relieved when Rhett announced he had an early day the next day and wanted to go to bed. Though, it broke my heart to see Sofia's smile fade as she reached for her glass of champagne and took a long swig.

For a second, I had the urge to tell her that Rhett and I weren't really in love, that we were just pretending, and that we were most certainly not rushing upstairs to have sex. Rhett was contractually hers. She didn't need to worry. Rhett wasn't mine to keep. Rhett wasn't mine to keep. Rhett...

"Parker, are you ready?" Rhett offered me his hand.

"Yeah," I blurted out. "I mean. Yes, we should sleep."

What? Ever since our kiss, I'd had this jittery energy surging through me. Everything Rhett said felt like a double entendre. I waved goodbye to the group, being careful not to make eye contact with Sofia. My heart pumped a million beats per second as I followed a tuxedo-clad Rhett out of the ballroom, down the corridor lined with Christmas trees, and up the grand staircase adorned with garland filled with frosted red berries, greenery, and large poinsettia flowers.

"Rhett, a word please." Gretchen appeared at the bottom of the stairs with Mark, the butler, right behind her. "Mark, would you mind?" She gestured toward me.

"Of course. I'll see Ms. Cruz to her room." He climbed the steps, stopping after he reached the top.

"I'll come check on you later." He kissed my cheek.

"Yeah, of course. Go." I offered Gretchen a weak smile, too tired to be overly polite.

I let Mark escort me down the wide hallway. I counted five doors on each side, which meant that either the Olde Windsor Gazette exaggerated on the size of the mansion, or I had really no idea how big this place was. Was there another wing to this place?

"I thought the upstairs would be bigger," I said while I stopped to admire one of the paintings on the wall.

"The west wing is for visitors. The east wing access is at the end of the corridor, last door on the right." He offered me a smile I could only describe as conspiratory.

"That makes more sense." I stopped to gaze at the next painting that looked like a portrait of Rhett but much older. "This place is incredible. It's almost like sensory overload."

"You get used to it." He stopped at the last door on the left.

Earlier tonight, I'd seen Sofia run upstairs to hide from her bodyguard. I assumed she'd come up here to hide in her suite. Knowing she wasn't staying in the East wing, possibly next to Rhett's room, was oddly satisfying.

"You should have everything you need." He opened the door and ushered me inside. "Sleep clothes, toiletries and fresh towels...it's all in the bathroom, through here." He opened another door on the opposite end of the room. "I took the liberty of starting a fire for you. The rooms can get chilly during the night. The furnace can only do so much."

"Thank you. It's all great. Wow." I strolled to the four-poster bed in the middle of the huge suite.

"If you need anything, just dial oo for housekeeping."

"Housekeeping, of course there's housekeeping." I plopped myself down on the plush mattress.

"Good night, Ms. Cruz."

"Good night, Mark. Thank you for everything." I waved with a huge smile on my face.

The door shut behind him. I sat there and took in the room —the intricate wood carvings on the fireplace mantle, the cozy sitting area in front of it, and the huge bed that would look ridiculously big in any other room. I tried to imagine Rhett living here. When we were in elementary school, I knew he lived at Windsor Mansion. But I never stopped to think about what that meant. Was he lonely? Even though Ava and her rowdy friends were still downstairs, I couldn't help but feel alone. The house was too quiet, too empty. For no reason at all, I pictured Rhett and Sofia with a bunch of kids in this house.

Now I understood why Rhett was so freaked out when he saw us on the cover of the Olde Windsor Gazette. He knew his aunt would have strong opinions about him dating, especially when his fiancée was in town for the holidays. Omigod, what a mess. I pressed my cold hand to my forehead.

Gretchen wasted no time offering me two million dollars to essentially break up with Rhett. Was that why she'd insisted

I spend the night? To make me see that she was right about how wrong I was for her great nephew? No doubt she had plans to keep me here until I agreed to let Rhett go. Crap. Our lie had gone too far. We had to come clean. I jerked to my feet and paced up and down the length of the bed as the idea gelled in my head. The truth was the only thing that could fix this whole mess we created. On the third loop around the area rug, I came face to face with a very confused Rhett.

"That didn't take long." I crossed my arms, then uncrossed them. I was so out of place.

"I was going to check on you. Did something happen?" He furrowed his brows and stepped closer.

"No. Why?" I met his gaze.

"Why are you here?" He shot a glance to the bed then the sofa facing the fireplace, before he smiled at the floor. "Mark. He brought you here."

"Yeah. It's a great room."

"I know. It's mine. My room." He released a breath as his eyes softened. "He brought you to my bedroom."

"Why would he think we would be sleeping in the same bed?" I stepped away from him.

"I swear I didn't ask him to." Rhett put his hands up in surrender.

"Oh no. I wasn't thinking that. I just um, it took me by surprise. I didn't think your aunt was the progressive, romantic type." I let out a nervous laugh.

"I don't think she is." He chuckled. "She thinks you're a soft spot—that having you here is going to make me change my mind."

That made sense. What better way to get a man in a pliable mood than to dangle sex in front of him? Wait, what?

No, Rhett and I were most definitely not having sex tonight. That would be utterly insane. And also, not part of our agreement.

"I'll call Mark and tell him we need a second bedroom." Rhett ambled toward the landline on the bedside table. "I'll just say we're trying to take things slow."

"If you do that, they'll know we're fake dating." I gripped the post. "I was thinking. Maybe this lie has gone far enough. Do you think..."

"Absolutely not." He dropped the phone on the cradle. "We can't tell anyone about our arrangement, especially not my great-aunt. That was the deal."

"I know. I was just thinking." I blew out a breath. "Tonight was intense."

"Yes, it was." He stuffed his hands in the pockets of his trousers and lowered his gaze. If that wasn't the look of a man who knew he'd been defeated, I didn't know what it would be. "I'm sorry. We never should've come here. I had no idea Sofia would be here. Though in retrospect, it was stupid of me to think that Aunt Gretchen would not use this opportunity to remind me of my duties."

Who would've thought that a tiny, innocent lie would turn into such a big deal. If I'd known, I never would've suggested it. Why did Rhett agree? I supposed that didn't matter. Regardless of how we got here, all we could do now was stick to our guns. Rhett was in hot water with his aunt and fiancée because of my great idea to fake date my boss. The least I could do was not humiliate Rhett by telling everyone the truth.

"Okay. This isn't a big deal." I gestured to the room at large. "Everyone knows that the solution to the one bed trope is a bunch of pillows."

"What trope?" He cocked an eyebrow.

"You know...there's two of us, one bed." My cheeks burned hot. Did I sound like I was thinking about sex? "I mean, I'm not saying we're going to have sex just because there's one bed. I mean, who does that, right? It's a stupid trope. It only works in romance novels."

He opened his mouth, but no words came out. "Were you...?" He trailed off. "Never mind, I can sleep on the sofa."

"Are you sure?"

"Yeah, it's just one night. I'll live." He cleared his throat. "You probably want to get out of that dress."

"Oh yeah. Mark said there were pajamas for me in the bathroom." I turned around and moved my hair out of the way. "Can you help me out?"

"Sure." His hot breath tickled the back of my neck just as his fingers brushed my skin.

He removed the diamond necklace first and set it on the bed. The room swayed a bit when he reached for the zipper and slowly pulled it down. How soon did he have to marry? And for how long? Gretchen's words flashed in my mind's eye, *there are worse things than being a Duke's mistress.* Who talked like that, honestly?

"Thanks." I gathered the long skirt and headed for the bathroom.

I closed the door behind me and leaned on it. Ignoring the fact that the room had gone up a million degrees, I let the dress drop to the marble floor, picked it up, then draped it over the towel rack. Next to the sink, I found the pajamas Mark had laid out for me. Well, pajamas weren't exactly the right word. I sniffed the garment before I pulled it over my head. Even though it was bright white and clean, it seemed old.

"This is awesome." I sighed, looking at myself in the mirror while I tied the lace at my neck into a neat bow.

"Is everything okay?" Rhett called out.

"Yeah. Coming." I put on the soft bedroom slippers and walked out.

Rhett had already changed out of his tuxedo and donned a pajama set that was totally normal and looked super-hot on him. "What are you wearing?"

"Gretchen hates me." I picked up the excess fabric on the nightgown. "I look like Ebenezer Scrooge." The irony was not lost on me.

Rhett laughed so hard; I was ready to punch him. A whole minute later, he managed to find his composure to ask. "Which adaptation?"

"Which adaptation?" I glanced down at my getup then up. "The one with Jim Carrey? All I'm missing is the hat."

"Well, did you look?" He pointed at the bathroom. When I advanced toward him with my fist in the air, he put up his hands in mock surrender. "You look adorable."

"I look ridiculous." I glared at him.

"Not even a little bit." His bright smile disarmed me.

I returned the gesture and got lost in his blue gaze. "I guess it doesn't matter what I wear to bed. It's just for one night. I'll live." I echoed his words from before.

"Right. Just one night." His grin faded as he shot a quick glance to the bed. "Are you hungry?"

I wasn't. But I was not ready to sleep in the same room as Rhett. After a three-hour meal, I doubt he was hungry either, but the fact that he offered made me think that maybe he wasn't ready for the night to end either. Jeez, between the one big bed and the Victorian-style nightgown, I was starting to feel like a virgin bride on her wedding night. Not that I was jealous, but Sofia was a lucky girl.

"I'm starving." I beamed at him. "What do you have in mind?"

"Well, by now, I'm sure the catering crew has gone home. Let's go roust around in the kitchen and see what we can find. We should have the place all to ourselves." He winked at me.

"Roust around?" I laughed.

"That's what my grandfather used to call it." He offered me his hand. "Are you in?"

"So in." I laced my fingers through his and ignored the rush of adrenaline that shot straight into my chest.

As we strolled down the long hallway, Rhett took the time to talk about the oil paintings hanging on the walls. The one portrait I had seen earlier turned out to be of his grandfather. The resemblance was uncanny. But when I mentioned it to Rhett, he shook his head in dismissal. What was it about his family that pained him so much?

The small party in the ballroom was still in full swing. Rhett placed his index finger to his lips, which to me, was the universal sign that we were now sneaking about. I nodded, and he ushered me past the stairs and toward the library, where he pulled open a door that matched the wallpaper and paneling as the rest of the wall. Of course the mansion came complete with secret passageways that led to the kitchen.

"Good evening. Rhett. Ms. Cruz." Mark stopped to greet us in the less ornate hallway. "Rousting around at this hour?"

"Habits die hard." Rhett shrugged. "Good night, Mark."

"Good night. Again." I waved at him as we continued down the long corridor and a set of stairs.

The kitchen was as big as the main floor of my Craftsman-style home. Like my house, the kitchen had rustic built-in shelving, cabinets and furnishings. On one side the twelve-burner stove served as the main focal point. The oversized fireplace on the opposite side balanced out the room. I loved old houses.

"Rhett." A woman in her late sixties rushed forward to hug him. "I was wondering if I'd see you tonight."

"Me too. These dinners are getting longer and longer." He quipped before he turned to me. "Abigail, this is Parker Cruz." He cleared his throat. "My, my girlfriend."

"Oh dear." Abigail grabbed both my hands while beaming at him. "It is so good to finally meet you, Parker."

"It's good to meet you too." I matched her energy, feeling guilty about lying to her.

Rhett and I had been fake dating for two days. How was she so excited for us? Maybe she didn't know about Sofia. That would be impossible though. Everyone here knew about Rhett's arranged marriage.

"You must be hungry." She patted Rhett's stomach. "Let me make you a sandwich."

"No, don't worry about it, Abi. It's late. Go to bed. We'll manage in here." Rhett winked at her.

"Of course." She smiled even bigger. "I'll leave you two alone."

"She's so nice." I said to her retreating form.

"She's the best. Her and Mom were best of friends when we lived here." He shook his head a bit as if dismissing old memories.

"Do you miss this place?" I asked.

"More than I realized." He sighed.

CHAPTER 12

Are You Sure?

RHETT

"You know what this fireplace is perfect for? Roasting chestnuts." Parker left my side and strode to the lively fire. "Oh, this feels nice." She put out one hand while she held her oversized Victorian-style nightgown away with the other. "Do you have any?" She stepped closer to the circle of light emanating from the fire and flashed me a perfect view of her body.

"I'm sure there are some in the pantry." I stood there like a creep, ogling the outline of her figure through the now semi-translucent fabric.

"Let's make some." She beamed at me.

What the hell was wrong with me? This entire night I had not been able to get Parker out of my mind. More than that, I couldn't stop thinking about our kiss. The fact that her hand spent the entire evening not two inches away from my cock didn't help matters. How did we get here? A week ago, Parker thought of me as public enemy number one, a Scrooge. Now she was in my house looking at me like...like I was hers.

I was sure Mark thought he was doing us a favor when he put her in my bedroom. As tempting as she was, I had to admit that Aunt Gretchen's plan had worked. Mainly because she was right about everything. Even if my last name wasn't Windsor anymore, I was still part of this family. I was the only one with the ability to take the reins, to ensure Windsor Media's longevity. To think otherwise made me the biggest, most selfish asshole, which I'd been for the past year and a half since I got the grand idea that I could be mayor of Winterstorm Village.

"What do you think?" Parker asked, furrowing her brows.

"Think about what?"

"We have a kick-ass fireplace; we must roast chestnuts over an open fire." She met my gaze and held her breath.

She'd been doing that all night, smiling at me, touching me every chance she got. She'd never done that before. No matter how hard I tried, I could never get on her good side. I always assumed her aversion to me had something to do with my family. But after today, I could see that wasn't the case. She hated me, for me.

"I'll check the pantry." I headed to the room in the back where I knew Abigail kept the raw chestnuts. I handed Parker the bag and tried not to think of all the times I roasted chestnuts by myself in this kitchen. "Here you are."

"Okay we need a cast iron pan and a knife." She leaned on the marble counter and waited until I fetched all the things she needed.

"You've done this before?" I studied her red cheeks and

full lips while she expertly scored each chestnut by cutting an X on the shell.

Her nervous energy was an aphrodisiac to me. She talked fast as she told the story of the last time her dad attempted to roast chestnuts with her. "I was ten. Mom had explicitly said not to use the fireplace. Dad did it anyway. I swear, not five minutes had gone by before the rug caught fire. It was a freaky accident. Totally not our fault. But still, Mom was so mad." She laughed.

"You miss her." I leaned across the island counter and moved a stray hair away from her face.

"It's worse around Christmas." She shrugged. "What about you? How can you miss a place that never left you."

"Aaand, she's back." I gathered the scored nuts, tossed them in the pan, and sprayed them with water.

"I'm sorry. That was harsh." She put the knife down. "But you know what I mean. This is your home. Gretchen offered me money to essentially get you to come back. Why won't you?"

I swallowed the lump in my throat. I had asked myself that same question a million times before. But looking at Parker now, basking in the serenity of her brown eyes, I realized why. "I wanted more than this."

"Yeah, you're right. This place is a total dump."

"I mean, more out of life." I chuckled. "Dad was never happy here. That's why Mom left. She didn't want me to grow up and be stuck here like Dad. He hated being tethered to the Windsor name. In turn, Mom hated the man he became when he was here. She married the fun, loving, live by the ocean guy. Not the city lawyer with a legacy to uphold."

"Oh." She ambled around the counter and placed her

hand on my shoulder. "So that's it? You're staying away, refusing to be a Windsor again because of your mom. She doesn't want you here."

"No, it's not like that. I don't feel guilty for being here." I glanced down at my hands.

"I didn't say guilty." She pointed her index finger at me in that infuriating way that said *I know you know I'm right.*

Of course she was right. I wanted to be here, to be officially all the things Aunt Gretchen wanted me to be. But then, what would I say to Mom? Sorry, you went through all that trouble to set me free.

"You sticking it to the Windsors is your way to stay loyal to her." She said mostly to herself, as if trying to truly understand my dichotomy. "I'm sorry."

"What do you have to be sorry for?" I turned to meet her gaze and leaned my hip on the edge of the counter.

"I always thought you were so pompous for leaving. I assumed you thought you were too good for this town." She slid her hand down to my chest.

"I knew it. You do hate me." My heart drummed hard against the spot where her fingers seared their mark on my skin.

"I don't. I guess. I guess I just expected more from you because you were a Windsor. Your family founded Winterstorm Village. How could you not care about it?" Her eyes watered for a moment before she glanced away.

I hadn't seen Parker cry since we were ten. Her mother had just passed, and I was leaving town. Back then, we were friends. Even though I couldn't imagine the kind of pain she was going through for losing her mom, I felt for her. I hated that she had to suffer on her own. My last day in town, I followed her to the cemetery after school. I hid behind an oak tree and watched her cry until I couldn't stand it anymore and went to her. When I sat next to her on the lawn, she leaned on my shoulder and sobbed. That day, I told her she wasn't alone. Even though I knew I was leaving for good, I promised her I would return. Did she remember?

"I do care, Parker. I've always cared. It's why I came back."

"Yeah, in the body of the most pompous person I'd ever met. I hardly recognized you." The fire in her eyes replaced her tears. "You hated everything about our school."

"I was embarrassed. Without the Windsor name, I didn't think I belonged here anymore." I shook my head, smiling at the memory of us when I thought that if Parker Cruz, the town's sweetheart liked me, I could belong again. "And you didn't waste a second to make sure I knew exactly how big of a pompous ass I was." I raised a brow. "What was it you called me?"

"Pfft. I don't remember." She shrugged.

"I think you do remember." I cocked my head to look her in the eye. "Something about a walrus?"

"A walrus with spectacles." She said under her breath while she grabbed the pan by the handle and placed it on the fireplace rack.

"That's it." I chuckled. "That doesn't even make any sense."

"I was fourteen, okay? I thought walruses looked very self-important." She pursed her lips to hide her smile, as she tossed the chestnuts a few times. "It didn't matter. Everyone loved you anyway. Even started calling you Parker, like you asked them to."

"I'm sorry about that. I was too much in my head back

then. I wasn't thinking about how that would make you feel." I closed the space between us.

"I was angry at everything and everyone back then." She sighed. "It took a long while to realize that when Mom died, I was the only one who lost her mom. Everyone else was fine because they didn't lose someone so important to them. They moved on. And I just couldn't."

"I broke my promise to you." I ran the back of my fingers across the apple of her cheek.

"I was hoping you'd forgotten about that." She leaned into my hand as her gaze lowered to my mouth. "We both became different people."

"Parker." I bent down and pressed my forehead to hers. "I'm still me."

"Are you sure?"

When I nodded, she came up on her tiptoes and pressed her lips to mine. Since the day we both agreed to this crazy fake dating ploy, we'd only touch or kissed when others were around. I had to keep myself in check every time. But now, Parker Cruz was in my arms. She wanted me, and for the life of me, I couldn't remember why being with her was such a bad idea to begin with. I deepened the kiss and walked her toward the kitchen island.

Desperate to feel her skin, I gathered the fabric of her nightgown and pulled it up to her waist. I cupped her butt cheek with both hands. As if we'd done this a million times before, she wrapped her legs around my waist while I propped her up on the counter. Hot blood rushed through me as I kissed every part of her I had access to. Somewhere in the recesses of my mind, I knew this dream would end soon. I never really understood how much I wanted her until now.

"Parker." I sucked on the cord of her neck, then moved down to her chest and inhaled her scent, rubbing my face on the swell of her breast.

"I'm here." She tunneled her fingers through my hair as my mouth found her taut nipples buried in the fabric of her nightgown. "Hmm."

Her moan tugged at the spot below my navel. I was so hard for her. And now we had a huge problem on our hands. I couldn't stop kissing her breasts and running my hands up and down her shapely legs. I couldn't make myself pull away. I could never let her go again. Even if it was an act before, Parker had it right. I was irrevocably hers.

I squeezed her hip tightly and brought her closer to my body. Her eyes flew open when my erection rubbed against her pussy. Her lips parted. Before she uttered a word, I captured her mouth again and kissed her with all the desire I felt bursting through my body. I needed her to know how she made me feel.

"Wait." She panted a breath.

I nodded and buried my face in her neck while I figured out how to fill my lungs with air again. After several beats, I stepped back. Something raw pulsed in my chest at the sight of her—swollen lips, pink cheeks, and heated skin. I'd never seen Parker turned on.

"You're right. We should stop." I met her gaze.

The lust in her eyes was enough to set my body on fire. I wedged myself between her legs and cradled her neck. Our hot breaths swirled between our mouths. I wanted to devour her right here and now.

"Omigod. Your chestnuts are burning." Sofia darted across the kitchen, grabbed an oven mitten off the counter, and pulled the cast iron pan out of the fireplace. "Where should I put it?" She held the pan at arm's length.

"Omigod." Parker jumped off the counter and pointed at the trivet behind her. "Just there."

"I think they're ruined." Sofia poked at them with her mitten. "Too bad. They smell so good." She paused, then slowly turned to face me. "I didn't mean to interrupt. You were..."

"No. You didn't interrupt. We were just saying how we should be going back upstairs." Parker swallowed. "To sleep. So. I'm gonna go. Good night." She waved at the two of us.

The minute Parker left the kitchen, cold air filled the room. I braced both hands on the edge of the counter and released a breath. When I lifted my gaze, I found Sofia looking at me with pity in her eyes.

"Over the years, I've seen you with a lot of women. This is the first time I see something different in you." She offered me a kind smile. "You're in love with her."

"What?" I scoffed. "It's getting late. I should get to bed. Good night, Sofia."

"Yeah, good night." She waved then turned her attention to the chestnuts.

On my way upstairs, I considered stopping by the ballroom to get a stiff drink. Maybe if I waited a while, Parker would fall asleep before I got back. The minute the thought entered my mind, all I could see was Parker naked in my bed. A clear image of me burying my face between her legs seared its way into focus.

At some point we had to talk about what almost happened in the kitchen. But tonight wasn't the time. I needed several cold showers before I could have a coherent conversation with

Parker. When I reached the bottom of the grand staircase, I realized that there was a high possibility that Parker might've gone home instead. My pulse became bolts of lightning again, not from wanting her so much. But from fear of losing her. I darted up the stairs and barged into my own room. Parker glanced up at me in surprise. She was still in her nightgown, which meant that maybe she didn't really want to leave.

"What are you doing?" I pointed at the red dress in her hands.

"I think I should go home." She inhaled. "I have work in the morning."

"Tomorrow is Sunday." I stalked toward her. "Your boss can't be that big of a hard ass to make you work on Sundays."

"He is, actually." She folded the dress neatly.

"Parker." I took the garment from her and set it on the edge of the bed. "Let's talk."

"About what?"

"This." I pointed at her and me.

I couldn't even bring myself to say the word...us.

CHAPTER 13

I Knew You'd Taste Good

Parker

I still hadn't recovered from the kitchen episode. Talking wasn't exactly what I wanted to do. What I wanted to do was go back in time and never ask Rhett to pretend to be my boyfriend. What the hell was I thinking? Why did I think that I could get close to him and not feel anything? He was Rhett freaking Windsor. Over the years, I'd seen him go through women like they're going out of style. Of course, now I knew why he could never allow himself to have feelings for them, but that didn't matter. Rhett couldn't be mine.

"I'm tired," I lied. "Let's just go to sleep."

"Okay." He nodded. "Tomorrow. Or whenever you feel like talking, I'll be here."

"Thanks." I sidestepped him to get to the right side of the bed.

He stood there and watched me toss the decorative pillows to the side, then turn down the covers. His disappointment filled the room. Or maybe that was me. Somewhere deep in my mind, I recognized that letting Rhett go tonight was something I was going to regret for the rest of my life. But what else could I do? Have hot sex with him, while his fiancée slept down the hall? Sure, he said he wouldn't marry her. To do that, he would have to become a Windsor first, which was something he couldn't do out of loyalty to his mom.

"Good night, Rhett." I faced him.

"Good night, Parker." He grabbed a couple of pillows from the left side of the mattress, then placed them on the sofa.

I made to climb under the covers, but then froze in place, as Rhett reached behind him and pulled off his pajama top. Panic mixed in with pent-up frustration bubbled to the surface. He glanced up at me, furrowing his brows. As if he didn't understand exactly how hot he was.

"What's wrong?" he asked.

"You can't sleep like that." I pointed at his perfectly-sculpted stomach. "You and your abs."

What did he do? Did he do a hundred pushups in the kitchen before coming here?

"I'll be under the covers." He pointed at the sofa. "On this side of the room."

"Is this my punishment for turning you down?" The words just spilled out of my mouth.

"Excuse me?" He stalked toward me, barefoot and with his abs flexing in all their glory. "You didn't turn me down. We were interrupted."

"After I stopped you." I stepped closer to him.

"Well, there you have it. You obviously are very good at resisting me. So what does it matter if I'm shirtless? I actually sleep in the nude. I'm wearing these pants for you." He braced both hands on his hips, as his chest swelled with every intake of air.

"Have you considered if it matters to Sofia?" I pointed toward the hallway.

He caught my hand and placed it on his bare chest. "Is that what this is about?"

"No."

"Parker."

"She thinks you're going to marry her," I blurted out.

"That's between her and Aunt Gretchen. I only want you," he whispered, and effectively brought down all my defenses.

The unravel happened the same way it had in the kitchen. The heat in the pit of my stomach burned its way up into my heart, and then my head where all logical thought just burst into tiny flicks of light. And that was it. Before I could think about consequences, I slid both my hands up into his hair and kissed him. The room swayed a few times before it came into perfect focus, with bright colors and the sweet scent of roasted chestnuts.

He took my mouth with such reverence; all I could do was melt into him. When I did, he reached for the hem of my nightgown and brought it up to my waist. The minute he palmed by butt cheeks, muscle memory kicked in. I wrapped my legs around him and pulled at his soft hair.

"Rhett." I meant it as a request. *Rhett, please be with me. Love me.*

"Are you sure?" He sat on the edge of the bed with me straddling him.

I nodded once and tugged at the satin ribbon. When the bow unraveled, the nightgown fell past my shoulder. With a soft moan, Rhett planted a kiss on my clavicle as he pulled the garment all the way down to my waist.

"Parker." My name on his lips sent a shiver down my spine. He wanted this too. "I don't have condoms here."

"I'm on the pill. It keeps the migraines away." No idea why I felt the need to explain myself. "I haven't been with anyone since before the campaign."

"I know." He brushed a strand of hair away from my face. "I haven't been with anyone since the debate."

"I know." I cupped his cheek. "I mean not that I was keeping tabs on you or anything. I..."

"I was." In one fluid motion, he rose to his feet, lay me on the bed, and removed the miles of fabric off me. He stepped back to admire my naked body. "You're so beautiful."

"So are you." I propped myself up on my elbows and openly ogled his abs and the bulge in his pajama pants. "Pants off."

He did as I asked. And omigod. Of course he was big. Before I told him just that, he knelt by the side of the bed and open-mouth kissed my pussy. His lips on me sent desire-induced adrenaline through my body that shocked me to my core. Every lap of his tongue along my seam, every ardent kiss, sent me higher up the climb. Having him between my legs felt like the most natural thing in the world.

"I knew you'd taste good." He blew a hot breath directly on my clit. "I want to see you come."

His admission was a surrender on his part. A cease fire. No more fighting. Just us. He worked me into such a heated frenzy that when I found my release, I more than came. I floated up into another dimension, where all I could feel were the waves of pleasure exploding from my center, searing every inch of my body, inside and out.

While I came down from my high, Rhett kissed my belly and slowly made his way up to my breasts. I ran my hands along his chest and abs as he pressed his erection to my entrance. I raised my hips to meet his, ready to take all of him.

"Not yet." He sucked hard on one taut nipple, then switched to the other. "Your skin is so soft." He buried his face between my mounds.

By now, the shockwaves of my previous orgasm had already dissipated, and I was hungry for more. I wanted him inside me in the worst way. I wanted to feel his fire.

"Don't hold back." I panted a breath. "I need this."

"I know." He captured my mouth again. When he came up for air, he cradled my cheek. "Look at me."

The lust I saw in his eyes fanned the flames in my core. Suddenly, my whole body was inundated with wave after wave of desire and pleasure. My clit ached for a bit of relief. Just when I thought I was going to explode, he took a handful of my ass and swelled into me in one swift motion. Jeez, the man was rock hard and so intense. My whole body hummed with raw energy from wanting him so much. When I tightened my walls around his cock, he let out a deep growly moan.

"You feel so good." He plunged even deeper.

He set a fast pace that showed me exactly how much he wanted me. How was it possible to fight with someone for so many years, and also, be this compatible? Being with Rhett was like nothing I'd ever experienced before. He was so intense and all-consuming. I didn't want this night to end. But it had to. I could feel my orgasm building again as he continued with his relentless rhythm of charging in and out of me.

As if he could sense that I was at the very edge, he took both my wrists and placed them over my head while his impressive body hovered over me. He pumped hard into me a handful of times, and then, I was floating again—I came hard and longer than before. Watching Rhett fall to pieces while moaning something that sounded like my name was my new favorite thing.

"Jesus. What the hell was that?" He buried his face in my breasts, while he labored to catch his breath.

I loved that I did that to him. That he completely unraveled because of me.

"Wow, you're really good at that." I ran my hands down his back, reveling in the weight of his body against mine.

We lay like that for several minutes while we came down from our high. The whole time a single question swirled in my head. I didn't want to ruin the moment, but I had to know. I'd crossed the line. I couldn't lie to myself anymore. I hated the idea of Rhett being with someone else. I realized now that all night, while Sofia monopolized his time, I was jealous.

I squeezed my eyes shut, then blurted the words flashing in my mind's eye. "What happens now?"

"What do you mean?" He lifted his head to look at me. "With us?"

"Yeah, the whole fake dating thing kind of went out the window the minute you saw my boobs."

"It kind of did, didn't it?" He laughed and then pulled a nipple into his mouth. "They are the most perfect boobs."

"Hmm." My eyes fluttered closed.

"I'd like to date you for real." He braced both hands on either side of my head. "What would you say are my chances?"

"Well, given how you're still inside me. I'd say really good."
I cupped his face. "What about…?"

"Don't say her name." He bent down to kiss me. "They
can't make me do something I don't want to do. Do you
trust me?"

I considered his question for several beats. To my surprise,
I realized that I did trust Rhett. Even though we didn't agree
on much in the office, I trusted that he wanted to do the right
thing. I believed him when he said he wanted to be with me.
And omigod, I wanted to be with him too. I wanted to wake up
next to him every morning. I wanted him to be mine.

"Yeah, I trust you." I smiled at him.

"Parker." He pressed his forehead to mine. "Of course you
had to drive me to the edge of insanity before we could get to
this point."

"I didn't know it could be like this." I pressed my lips to
his. "Do you have something to ask me?"

"Make it official? Okay." He climbed off me and pulled me
off the bed. "Parker Cruz, do you want to be my girlfriend?"

I chuckled. Something in the way he posed the question
made me feel like we were kids again. For a moment, I
wondered what our lives would've been like if he hadn't left
town all those years ago. Maybe we were always meant to end
up together. This was the craziest idea ever. But at the same
time, being here with Rhett felt like the most natural thing in
the world.

"Yes." I wrapped my arms around his torso. "I want to be
your girlfriend."

"I hope you don't have plans for tomorrow." He glanced
down at his erection for a beat.

"Why's that?" I wrapped my fingers around his hard as steel shaft and gave it a few pumps.

"Because I plan to make love to you all night." He said through gritted teeth.

"Zero plans." I stood on my tippy toes and kissed him.

"Parker." He growled softly against my lips.

Yeah, watching Rhett lose all composure while moaning my name was my new favorite thing.

The next morning, after three more rounds of mind-blowing sex, I woke up wrapped in Rhett's arms. Everything about him felt like home. He felt right. I snuggled closer to him. Out in the hallway, Ava's voice carried into the room. I could only assume all the guests were waking up and gathering downstairs for brunch. Was I ready to face Sofia's super nice face this morning? Not even a little bit. It was one thing to pretend to be dating his fiancée, and a whole other thing to sleep with him.

Rhett had said he had no intention of marrying her. But that didn't change the fact that for several years Sofia had thought of him as hers. My heart raced at the idea of going downstairs to share a meal with her and make polite conversation. I groaned quietly and moved away from Rhett. When he didn't move, I grabbed his pajamas off the floor and put them on. They were huge on me, but they were warm, and best of all, they had Rhett's scent.

I padded to the bathroom to wash up, while I considered my options. If I told Rhett how I felt about seeing Sofia, I had no doubt he would kiss me, and then, I would end up staying. I couldn't stay. When I finished brushing my teeth, I grabbed my phone and texted Ava.

Me: need a huge favor

Ava: anything

Me: I need a ride asap. I'll explain later

Ava: sure. Meet out front? Everyone is in the dining room

Me: thank you!!!!!!!!

As I looked around the room to make sure I had everything, my gaze kept going back to Rhett. He had the covers up to his waist. Somehow, he'd gotten more handsome in the last few days. Crap. I had to get out of here before my resolve crumbled and I crawled back into bed with him. I donned my coat, then picked up Ava's dress and draped it over my arm. For a moment, I considered going barefoot, but it was freezing out there. With a wince of shame, I slipped on my high heels, which totally clashed with Rhett's pajama set.

I said a quiet goodbye to Rhett, then walked out. Once I left Rhett's bedroom, I rushed down the grand staircase and out the massive front door. As soon as I reached the outside, I spotted Ava standing next to Mark and a limo.

"I forgot to mention that I didn't want anyone to know," I said to Ava before I waved at Mark. "Good morning. I have to go into the office."

"Of course, the driver will take you anywhere you wish." He opened the door for me.

"I'm sorry." Ava hugged me. "Mark was our only option."

"It's fine. Thank you for helping me." I glanced back toward the mansion, half expecting Rhett to appear by the door.

When I didn't see him, I climbed into the back of the limo and sat back. As the car slowly rolled away, I turned again to see the mansion one last time. I was a total chicken shit, I knew that. But I just wasn't ready to face the reality that now Rhett and I were a real thing.

CHAPTER 14

He Never Stopped

Parker

"Oh yeah, here you go." I tapped my phone to the card reader to pay for my coffee.

"Are you okay?" Sam laughed. "I asked if you wanted a blueberry muffin with your coffee."

"I'm sorry. Yeah, I'll take a muffin." I rubbed the side of my face. "I didn't get much sleep last night."

"You don't say. Go sit down. I'll bring you your coffee." He gestured toward the table by the window, where Briar and Rowena were practically bouncing in their seats waiting for me.

They wanted details about the party and my new relationship with Rhett. But I wasn't ready. It was all too new, too fast, too intense.

After I snuck out of Windsor Mansion this morning, I went straight home and slept a few hours before I visited Dad at the hospital. Before checking my messages, I considered crawling back into bed, maybe calling Rhett to see if he wanted to join me. But news traveled fast in this town. The minute I stepped out of Dad's room, I received a slew of texts from my friends.

Briar: Parker has been spotted!

Rowena: what? where?

Briar: Ava just texted. P is on her way home

Sam: she survived the mansion

Sam: guuurrrlll...check in

Rowena: coffee shop NOW

Briar: On my way!

Rowena: where is she?

Briar: Parker. Parker. Parker

Me: comiiiiing

As soon as Briar saw me coming, she pulled out a chair and patted the seat. "How's your dad? Mrs. Birdwhistle said she saw you at the hospital."

"He's getting there." I sat. "He might come home next week."

"That's great news. Just in time for the SnoBall." Rowena beamed at me, then reached over to help Sam set a tray of coffees on the table. "How is that coming along anyway?"

"Well, we're still short on funds. But I still need to check in with a few people who said they might be able to donate money. We'll get there." I sipped from my peppermint mocha.

"One second." Sam put up his index finger. "Don't start without me. I gotta grab the blueberry muffin."

"Take your time." I was okay with waiting.

If it were up to me, I would put off this debrief indefinitely. Or at least until I had a better idea what kind of relationship Rhett and I had. Debriefing the girls after a date got started back in middle school after I went to my first dance. Even after we all left for college, we continued our tradition via texts or video calls. Looking at my friends' eager faces, I realized that we hadn't had a debrief session in over two years.

Since Rowena returned from college, she had been focused on getting the coffee shop off the ground. Same with Briar, who'd been working tirelessly to keep her family's old Christmas Tree farm going. And then, there was me. I hadn't dated anyone since way before Dad's campaign started.

I wanted to tell them everything about Rhett. Except our date hadn't been a normal date. I went to dinner at Windsor mansion with Rhett as his fake girlfriend. Even though the night ended with us being boyfriend-girlfriend officially, I still wasn't sure if a relationship with Rhett had any real future.

"Okay." Sam placed a muffin on a plate in front of me. "Tell us everything."

"The party was like nothing I've ever experienced. Every-thing was over the top." I bit into the muffin. "It was like being inside *A Christmas Carol* movie."

"Ava said you looked spectacular in your red dress. Of course, Rhett was an extra shot of hot in his tux." Briar sipped from her cup quickly, then added, "She also mentioned you and Rhett looked so in love."

"We did?" I let out a nervous laugh. This whole charade of fake dating Rhett only to start dating him for real had me so confused. "It's a little early for that." I waved my hand in dismissal. "It's too soon for love."

Was it possible for someone like Rhett to fall in love with me? Sure, he wanted me. That much I knew for sure. But love was an entirely different thing. Wasn't it?

As soon as the question popped into my head, Rhett appeared at the end of the street, looking incredibly hot in a pair of jeans, cashmere sweater, and boots. A dark double-breasted long coat completed his impeccable aesthetic.

"Speak of the devil." Sam squeezed my arm. "He's delicious. Oh wait. He's heading our way. Act normal."

Rhett took long strides then reached for the door handle. The half smile pulling at his lips told me he knew he was the topic of conversation this morning. I beamed at him as flashes of him moaning my name fluttered through my mind.

He returned the gesture, stopping just a couple of feet from our table. Adrenaline and desire rushed through my body then settled at my core the moment his signature scent hit me square in the face.

"I woke up, and you were gone." His voice broke the silence.

Omigod. Did he just tell all my friends that we slept together? I shifted my gaze to their stunned faces. Crap. Now they knew Rhett and I had sex. I jumped to my feet.

"Come with me." I pulled him by the hand to the other side of the coffee shop. "What did you just do?" I whispered as soon as we were far enough away from my friends' prying ears.

"What do you mean?" He furrowed his brows, as if he truly didn't know what he just did.

"You told them." I gestured toward my friends.

"That you left this morning without saying goodbye?" He reached for my hand and placed it on his chest. "I understand why you felt you needed to leave. But I could've come with you. You texted Ava? You could've asked me for a ride."

"I panicked." I slid my fingers down to his abs. "I couldn't face them. Your aunt and Sofia."

"You're not having second thoughts, are you?" He cradled my neck.

"No." I sighed and leaned into him. "Last night was incredible. But I don't know what I'm doing."

"I know what you mean. It all feels big." He ran the pad of his thumb over my lips. "All I know is that I'm not giving up on you." He bent down and captured my mouth in a searing kiss.

"They're kissing." Sam made a sound like a high-pitched squeal.

"We should probably take this somewhere else." He stopped kissing me but didn't let me go. "Can I see you tonight? So we can talk about...us."

"Yeah." I released a breath. "No. I mean. I can't. I promised Mrs. Birdwhistle I would be there tonight for dress rehearsal. She's doing a fundraiser for us."

"I heard about that." He smiled. "Someone told her I'd be willing to play the role of Scrooge. Do you know anything about that?"

"I was mad at you for cutting my Christmas budget to pieces." I pointed toward the town square. "This beautiful wonderland doesn't happen by accident. It requires money."

"I know that. I saw your proposal." His eyes did that smoldering thing.

"They found a Scrooge. So you're off the hook." My knees buckled into each other. All of a sudden, all I wanted to do was go home and tear off his clothes. I slipped my hands under his sweater and ran my fingers across his hot skin. "Maybe we can meet afterward. My place?"

"I would like that." His chest swelled up as he peeked at something behind me. "I should let you get back to your friends."

"Okay." I nodded. "You probably have things to do."

He leaned in, and I closed my eyes. But instead of kissing

me like I'd expected, he pressed his lips to my forehead. That was probably the smart thing to do. I was so close to asking him to come back to my house right now. Why couldn't we do that?

"I do have things to do. I promised Aunt Gretchen I would go shopping with her." He dipped his head in the direction of the town square. "She's waiting for me."

I turned around and immediately spotted her and Sofia. I swore I wasn't the jealous type. But I really hated the idea of Rhett spending time with Sofia.

"I promise, you're the only one I want," he whispered in my ear.

"I wasn't thinking about that." I shrugged as if I didn't care that my boyfriend had a date with his fiancée. Argh, what a mess. "Go. Have fun."

"I'll see you tonight." He surveyed my face for a beat then sauntered toward the door, waving to my friends on the way out.

"Nice to see you, Mr. Mayor," Sam said before turning to me. "I know you're a lady. And you don't kiss and tell. But I have to know. Does he smolder in bed?"

The image formed in my head before I could stop it. The memory of Rhett's intense gaze as he orgasmed was forever tattooed on my soul.

"He does." I plopped myself on the chair and dropped my head on the table a little too hard. "Ow." I rubbed my forehead where he'd kissed it.

"That good, huh?" Briar laughed. "Look at you. You're all red."

"I've never had sex like that before." I took in a breath. "He made me feel...I don't know. Worshipped." I pressed my palms to my hot cheeks.

"Well, that makes sense." Rowena nodded. "That boy has been in love with you since the fifth grade."

"What?" I sat up. "What did you just say?"

"Um." Rowena cleared her throat. "What did I say?"

"The thing." I couldn't say the word love.

"That you guys. You know." She waved her hand toward the Arabelle.

"No, I don't know." My gaze darted from Sam to Briar, then back to Rowena.

"Come on. Everyone knows." Rowena looked to Briar for support.

"Wait. Everyone? What? Okay." My head felt like it was about to explode. "Who in their right mind would think Rhett is in love with me?"

One by one, Rowena, Briar, and Sam raised their hands.

"What?" was all I could say.

My brain froze. This was impossible. For as long as I could remember, Rhett and I have been mortal enemies. Okay, maybe we didn't exactly hate each other. But we did dislike each other a lot...fighting in public was literally our thing.

"We can't stand each other." I finally found a more convincing argument. "We fight all the time."

"I thought that was like your guys' kink." Sam shrugged and pointed at Rowena. "Right?"

"I thought it was more like a shield they used to protect each other," Rowena added.

Briar interjected, nodding, "Yeah, you know because he's royalty and stuff."

"He's not royalty." I slapped Sam's hand, so he'd put it down, then Briar's. "Omigod. This whole time you thought I was in love with him and you didn't tell me? I'm so embarrassed." I took the muffin and stuffed it in my mouth. "For the record, I'm not in love with him."

"Okay." Briar sipped from her coffee, then mumbled, "But he is."

"You don't know that," I blurted out. "You can't know that."

"Well." Rowena raised one eyebrow. "I can see why you wouldn't want to see it. It's intense. You guys are like fire on fire. But if you think about it. He's always there when you need him."

"He took the deputy job after he lost." Briar met my gaze with so much pity in her eyes.

"Think of all the coffees he's stolen from you," Sam said as if coffee was the definitive proof.

"It's because he insists on going by Parker...which...is my first name." I pointed at the letters scribbled on my cup, though the usual annoying feeling in my stomach wasn't there.

I couldn't see the grumpy boss anymore, only Rhett. Rhett showing up late at night to the hospital to check in on me and Dad.

"*I came because you called.*" He'd said when I accused him of being there to steal Dad's job.

Rhett was also there at the cemetery, just sitting there with me so I wouldn't be alone. He came back to Winterstorm Village because he cared.

I do care, Parker. I've always cared. It's why I came back.

I thought about our first kiss. A real fake boyfriend would've avoided the situation altogether. He could've used any number of excuses to stay away from me. Instead, he took my breath away.

"She's right." Sam patted my hand. "Mrs. Parker Parker? That was never going to work out."

"Also, he has to marry sweet, perfect Sofia." Briar shrugged.

"No, he doesn't," I snapped at her, suddenly feeling like I needed to sleep for at least a week. "He's not a Windsor. And he doesn't want to be. So there." I squinted at her. "And how do you know so much about the engagement and Sofia?"

"Me?" Briar turned bright red. "Um. Ava told me. She said the marriage was arranged between the two families when Sofia was seven. Sofia's family is bringing in like a lot of money to Windsor Media. It's like two media giants coming together. It's a really big deal."

"But Rhett P. Windsor doesn't exist." I raised my voice to make my point. "Rhett Parker wants me."

The minute the words spilled out of my mouth, I realized what I had just admitted without admitting it. I was in love with Rhett. As much as I'd like to deny it, I was also one hundred percent the jealous type. I didn't want him to marry Sofia. I wanted him for me. Just me.

"Gretchen offered me money to let him go. To talk him into taking the Windsor name again, the fortune, and the princess." I slouched and dropped my head again on the table with a big thud.

After a round of gasps, Rowena rubbed my arm. "You're in love with him, aren't you?"

"Never," I mumbled. After several beats, I said aloud what I already knew to be true. "Yes."

"Omigod." Briar jumped out of her seat and rushed around the table to hug me. "Of course you are. And now we can work on a plan to get rid of Sofia."

"I like how your brain works." Sam slapped the table. "Now how does one make a princess disappear? We're here for you, P."

"No, guys, we can't do that. She's super nice and madly in love with Rhett. It's why I left this morning. I just couldn't face her sweet face. She's like this perfect Disney princess. I bet singing birds and mice follow her around." I sat back to look at my friends. "Am I too late?"

"It's never too late," Rowena said.

"He never stopped loving you," Briar added.

"Mrs. Parker Parker. Are we sure? Alright." Sam winked at me. "What are you going to do, gurl? How can we help?"

Rhett wanted to be with me. He didn't care that his family had plans for him. None of it mattered because his mom made sure Rhett wasn't bound to whatever messed up contract his dad agreed to on his behalf. Rhett was free to choose. He chose me.

"I'm going to tell him." I beamed at them. "I'm going to tell him I love him."

CHAPTER 15

The Choice was Easy

Rhett

Would it be considered stalking my own girlfriend if Mrs. Birdwhistle personally invited me to her students' dress rehearsal? Earlier today, I had every intention of giving Parker space to digest everything that'd happened after dinner. I had to admit, the entire night took me by surprise too. Never in a million years would I have thought that Parker and I would end up officially dating, and then sleeping together.

The whole thing seemed far-fetched, maybe a little ridiculous because Parker and I were the complete opposite of two people who would fall for each other. Parker Cruz was Ms. Christmas cheer in a bottle. I was, rightly so, the Scrooge of this town.

I glanced up at the high school auditorium. The banner for the new play this week had already been hung up. I found it suspicious that even though Parker's budget had been severely cut, a lot of the Christmas activities around town were still scheduled as planned. Did she really believe that a high school play could save Christmas? That it would make enough money to pay for her sixty-foot Christmas tree, the gingerbread house contest, the decorations, and the slew of items Parker considered vital to executing a proper holiday season?

I scoffed to myself. Of course she did. That was the essence of who Parker Cruz was. She believed in hope. She believed in this town and its people. What the hell was I thinking letting her rope me into this deranged idea of dating each other to save Christmas? I didn't need to say it aloud to hear how insane it was.

The same insanity that compelled me to say yes to her dating idea was the one that brought me here tonight. I wanted to help her. I was willing to do anything in my power to see her smile again. Not because I was the selfless type, but because I wanted Parker to smile at me, only me.

"Mr. Mayor." Mrs. Birdwhistle propped open the door to the auditorium lobby. "You came. Please come in. It's freezing out there."

"Thank you. I thought I'd stop by for a minute and see how the play is coming along."

"My kids are very talented. We're almost sold out. Which reminds me, did you get your tickets?" She ushered me inside then let the door close behind us. "Parker said you needed twenty-five for the whole office."

"She said that. Did she?" I chuckled.

"Yes, let me go find them for you. You can just scan the code here to pay." She pointed at a laminated paper stuck to one of the columns. "When you're done, come into the auditorium to get some hot chocolate."

"I will. Thanks." I scanned the QR code and began the process to pay.

"Hey." Parker stood at the double doors to the auditorium.

I glanced up from my phone. "Hey."

"What are you doing here?"

"Paying for my tickets." I showed her my phone as proof. "Apparently you told Mrs. Birdwhistle that I wanted to invite everyone at city hall."

"That does sound like something I would say to stick it to my grumpy boss." She beamed at me. "Come on. It's for a good cause."

"A Norway Spruce Christmas tree is not even a cause." I cocked an eyebrow.

"Proceeds will also go toward fixing the Olde Windsor." She slapped my stomach.

"Exactly how much money do you think you're going to make here? This isn't Broadway." I took her hand and placed it on my chest.

"It's better, actually." She slid her hand down to my abs then around my waist.

"Hmm." I inhaled her perfume.

That right there. That smile and that look were the reasons why I was in this mess. In all these years, I hadn't figured out how to say no to Parker. Even now I had an incessant urge to tell Mrs. Birdwhistle that I wanted to buy however many tickets she had left.

I cradled her neck and bent down to kiss her. From last night to tonight, we had gone from co-workers to people who made out at random places. She parted her lips, and I accepted the invitation, pushing my tongue past her teeth. She tasted of chocolate and peppermint.

Before I could consider the time or the place, I walked backward and pulled her toward me. When my back reached the wall, I turned with her in my arms and caged her with my body. Her moan ignited the usual spark below my navel. And just like that, I spiraled down the Parker rabbit hole.

"Your skin is so soft," I whispered on her lips then moved down to her neck.

"Omigod." She panted a breath, gripping the lapel of my coat. "Wait. There's...there's like a bunch of kids in there. And you're the mayor."

"You're right. Sorry." I stopped kissing her, laboring to catch my breath. "I should go."

"No, don't go. A bunch of us are going to the Jolly Wreath after rehearsals. Come with us." She bit her bottom lip. "If you want."

"I want." I cradled her cheek. "How can I say no when you ask so nicely?"

I stood there, studying her beautiful face for a whole minute before Mrs. Birdwhistle came back with my tickets.

"Oh, Parker. I see you found him." She placed her hand on her chest as if seeing us together was the most romantic thing she'd ever seen. "We're so happy for you."

"We?" I asked.

"You know." She waved in the general direction of the auditorium. "Here are your tickets." She handed me an envelope with "Mr. Mayor" written on the front of it.

"Thank you." I took it and stuffed it in the inside pocket of my coat.

"The office is going to love this play." Parker pulled me inside the auditorium and ushered me to the front row. "Guys, look who I found."

"Mr. Mayor." Sam waved with a big grin on his face. "Good to see you again."

"Hey." Rowena got up and made everyone scoot over to make room for me. "Thor is here too." She looked around. "Or was. Anyway, sit. Actually, grab a cup of hot cocoa first. I made it myself."

"It's really good." Parker ambled to the table set up next to the stage and poured a cup. "Try it. I already had like three."

I took a sip. "It's so good. Thanks."

"It's starting. Sit." Parker plopped herself beside Rowena, then pulled me down to take the seat next to hers.

Mrs. Birdwhistle came out on stage to present her students, while I did my best to ignore Parker's sweet perfume. Dramatic music spilled from the speakers above us as the curtain rose to reveal an eerie and snowy scene. Next to me, Parker uttered a small gasp. The white snow, the lamp post and small shop decked with garland and sprays were enough to suck her into the story.

"That's so good, right?" Parker asked Rowena before she turned to me. "I told you they were good. I was little Timmy my senior year."

"I know." I took her hand and kissed it. "You were an adorable little boy."

"I know." She bumped her shoulder to mine. "Pay attention. Your line is coming up."

"My...?" I stopped talking when Scrooge stood behind his desk and said, "Bah Humbug."

Parker placed a hand over her mouth to stifle her laugh. "Uncanny," she teased.

"Guys, shhh it." Rowena glowered at us.

The play continued with fairly elaborate scenery that I hadn't expected to see in a high school play. When it ended, we all stood to offer them a well-deserved round of applause. Mrs. Birdwhistle gave us a quick nod of appreciation then immediately proceeded to give her students pointers on what to change for opening night.

"She still terrifies me," Briar mumbled from the row behind us.

"She's super nice. She cares, that's why she's tough." Parker shifted her body to talk to Briar. "Are you joining us for drinks?" she asked.

"Yeah, that's why I'm here." She shot to her feet. "Let's go."

"I'll drive." I stood and waited for Parker to join me so we could all walk out together.

"How was shopping with Gretchen and Sofia?" Parker asked as I pulled into a spot across from the tavern. "I hope they bought a lot of stuff. We need their patronage."

"I made sure of it." I winked at her.

"Really? Are we talking at least a thousand a piece?"

"Just about."

"You're a better mayor than I thought you'd be." She beamed at me.

"Should I be offended by that?" I turned to the back seat to look at Briar, Rowena, and Sam.

"A little." Rowena shrugged.

"Not at all," Briar and Sam said in unison.

"Are they okay?" I asked Parker.

"Yeah, why?" She opened the car door and climbed out.

Once inside, Parker strode up to the bar to greet Joe. "The usual?" he asked with stars in his eyes.

The Jolly Wreath Tavern was Parker's favorite bar. I was sure she loved it because the place celebrated the holidays all-year round. From the music to the decorations, inside Joe's bar, it was Christmas eternal. I'd always wondered if Joe bought the bar because he loved Christmas or because Parker did.

"Yes, please." She smiled at him then turned her attention to the group. "Little girls' room." She mouthed.

"We're going with her." Rowena patted me on the shoulder. "I'll have my usual too."

"Me too." Briar filed past me.

"Same." Sam followed behind them.

"So the rumors are true." Joe placed an espresso martini in front of me and got to work on the next drink. "You and Parker, huh?"

"Yeah." I sat on a barstool and fished out my wallet from the inside pocket of my coat.

"Drinks are on me." Joe waved his hand in dismissal.

"I'm paying for my girlfriend's drinks. And her friends." I glared at him as I presented him my credit card.

He stood there meeting my gaze for a whole minute before he conceded and took my card. "Of course, Mr. Mayor."

Joe had had a thing for Parker since we were in high school. He wasn't her type, but that never stopped him from buying her drinks or hugging her every chance he got. Of course, Parker was clueless about his feelings. She thought of him as a friend. I knew that. So why the hell did it bother me so much that he felt like he could buy her things?

"Oof." Thor pulled out the barstool next to me and sat. "I get that you're going for jealous boyfriend vibes, but this—" He gestured to my entire body. "—this is more of a stalker-slash-serial killer vibe. I know they dated but ease up."

"What?" I furrowed my brows at him, shaking my head. "They didn't date. They went to prom together. It was more of a friend date." I stopped talking when Thor pressed his lips together to suppress a laugh. "Jesus, whatever you're here to say, just get it over with."

"Hey, Joe. How are you?" Thor smiled politely at Joe, then put up two fingers. "Two whiskeys neat, please."

"Coming right up." Joe nodded as he placed my check and card on the counter for me to sign.

Two minutes later, he returned with the whiskeys, two margaritas and a glass of red wine, before he ambled around the bar to clear out tables. I studied his form and the self-assured way he made quick work of placing dirty glasses on a tray, then wiping down each tabletop.

"As a friend." Thor leaned forward to block Joe from view. When I shifted my attention to him, he continued, "I'm glad that after all this time you finally get to scratch that itch. But—"

"Parker is not an itch. And you know that." I scowled at him. "You've been hanging around Aunt Gretchen for too long. You might want to take a break."

"Okay fine." He put up his hands in mock surrender. "She's not an itch. But she's also not your future. You must see that."

"You agree with my aunt then?" I asked. "She thinks that now that I've scratched 'the itch' that I will be able to move on and do the right thing."

"People like us, Rhett, we don't get to choose."

"People like us?" I cocked an eyebrow.

"Okay that sounded melodramatic, but you know it's true. Sooner or later, you're going to have to recognize that being a Windsor isn't a choice." He met my gaze.

I couldn't deny the honesty I found in his eyes. Thor was my friend. He meant well. But he couldn't even begin to understand how I felt. What Parker and I had was real. It was the kind of thing that couldn't be denied.

"We have to choose family above all else." He sipped his drink.

"I made my choice years ago. I'm not going back, Thor. Especially not now." I took a long swig of whiskey.

Across the way, Parker appeared in my line of sight. As soon as she saw me, she beamed at me, all red cheeks and sparkling eyes. Joe stopped with a big tray propped on his shoulder to look at her then me. I understood exactly how he felt. For years, all I could do was admire her from a distance. Until now. A smile pulled at my lips as I watched her close the space between us.

"Hi." She stopped inches from me.

"Hi." I wrapped my arm around her waist and pulled her toward me.

"Is this for me?" She reached across and grabbed her martini. She took a small sip, then another before she moaned quietly. "Joe," she called out. "This is perfection. Thank you. You're the best."

"You're welcome." He nodded once then resumed tapping on his ordering system screen.

Under the counter, Thor kicked my boot. When I glanced up, he mouthed the words, "serial killer vibes."

I rolled my eyes, then stood to offer Parker my seat. She made to sit but stopped when she spotted Briar returning from the bathroom with a little girl next to her.

"Hey." She pulled me aside. "Did you know Thor had a daughter?"

"What? No, I didn't." I turned to Thor, who was already at attention waiting for Briar and the little girl to come to him.

"Father, I'm ready to go home." The little girl was a mini, female version of Thor.

"Yes, let's go." He patted his pockets a few times, before he finally met my gaze.

"Father?" I asked.

"Right. Let me introduce you." He placed a hand on her shoulder. "Rhett, meet my daughter, Charlotte Eloise Marie Van Bardeleven. And yes, that is her real name. We met a week ago. It's a long story."

"Wow. I mean, hi. It's great to meet you, Charlotte." I shook the little girl's hand.

"The pleasure is mine, Mr. Rhett," she said formally then turned to face Thor. "Father?"

"Yeah, let's go." Thor waved goodbye. On his way out, he stopped in front of Briar and said, "Thank you."

"It was nothing." She shrugged, then winked at Charlotte.

"You really didn't know?" Parker asked as soon as the entrance door shut behind Thor and his daughter.

"If Thor didn't know, how could I have known?" I reached for my tumbler and sipped the rest of the whiskey.

Thor had a daughter? Was that what he'd meant when he said, "people like us"? Except, our situations were completely different. Thor couldn't walk away from his own blood. I, on other hand, owed Sofia exactly nothing. She wasn't family.

Parker was my home. The choice was easy. When it came to Parker, the choice had always been easy.

"You got so pensive?" Parker placed her hand on my chest. "What are you thinking?"

"Can I give you a ride home?"

CHAPTER 16

Don't Say It

Parker

I sat in Rhett's car fighting the jittery energy in my belly. Had he asked to drive me home because he wanted to talk or spend the night? I wanted to talk about us, but I had to admit, I hadn't stopped thinking about our night together since I left Windsor mansion this morning. I one hundred percent wanted a repeat of that. But did he?

As soon as he parked in front of my house, the air crackled with our unfulfilled desire. By the way he shifted his weight slightly in his seat, I could only assume he felt it too. This raw attraction between us was so hard to believe. Though it wasn't as far-fetched as Rowena's words from this morning.

That boy has been in love with you since the fifth grade.

This beautiful man could not have possibly been in love with me all this time. How did I not see it? Probably because it wasn't true. Sure, we had crazy hot sex last night, but that didn't mean anything. Love was a completely different thing.

"Do you want to come inside?" I blurted out. My cheeks

burned hot because in my head that question sounded completely inappropriate. "I mean. Do you want to have a drink with me? In the house? Inside?"

"I would like that." He flashed me a sexy smile that totally said he knew exactly what I was thinking.

"Great." I pushed the car door open and climbed out.

I rushed up the stairs. After a few tries, I managed to get the key in the lock. Rhett had been in my house a handful of times before. But this time felt different. My whole body was aware of his presence just a few feet behind me.

"You finally got your Christmas lights up." Rhett stood just off my porch, admiring the colorful lights strung along the roof.

"Oh yeah, Joe stopped by this morning to finish up. I told him not to, but he wanted to get them done before Dad came home." I turned the latch and pushed the door open.

"Of course. He's so helpful." He rolled his eyes as he sauntered into the foyer.

"Excuse me?" I chuckled. "Are you...are you jealous of Joe?"

"What? Of course not." He shut the door and wrapped his arms around my waist. "He tries so hard though."

"What do you mean?" I peered up into his eyes, keenly aware of his large hand on my lower back, holding me possessively.

I never would've pegged Rhett, Mr. Cool as ice, for the jealous type. He was totally wrong about Joe. Sure, Joe and I had been friends since kindergarten. For years, he was even part of our group until he decided he wanted to start his own band. After that he just didn't have time for us.

"He's into you. You haven't noticed?" He cocked his head to look me in the eyes.

"There's nothing to notice. He's just a friend who decided to help me with my Christmas lights this year."

"And who likes to buy you drinks all the time." He scoffed.

"Omigod. You really are jealous." I laughed.

I met his broody gaze. It was the same disgruntled look he would shoot my way every time Joe and I would talk. More than once, I noticed Rhett leave his seat and stride across the bar, seemingly in our direction. Only to stop and greet someone else. How could I have been so blind? All this time, Rhett had feelings for me. Why didn't he say something? Why fight with me day in and day out instead?

My chest hurt for him, and for all the times we'd wasted being angry at each other. Or rather, pretending to be. Because if I had to be honest, part of my discontent with him was that he was the only one in town who didn't find me the least bit charming. As the mayor's daughter, I was sort of the town's pet. I'd be lying if I said I didn't enjoy the attention. Everyone loved me, except Rhett.

"Do you love me?" I stepped back and braced myself.

"What?" He let out a low chuckle. "What do you mean?"

"I mean, are you in love with me?"

He glanced up and released a breath. I stood there and waited for him to make up his mind. Maybe Rowena was wrong. Maybe all the little clues I'd conjured up in my head since this morning were not real. Maybe the last few days were just a fluke. He cared about this town as much as I did. So why not go all in and pretend we're in love, just like we'd agreed. Yeah, that made so much more sense than Rowena's ridiculous idea that Rhett had been in love with me since we were kids.

He shook his head and glanced at me with a silent, *I'm sorry.*

Well crap.

"You know what? Don't answer that. It was a stupid question." I cleared my throat. "Can I get you something to drink? Red wine? You like red wine, right?" I dashed to the kitchen to look for something to wash down the bitter taste in my mouth.

I was a complete idiot for thinking that Rhett might be in love with me. Me and my big mouth. Why couldn't I just let the fantasy be? Why did I have to ask him straight up? I uncorked a bottle of wine, grabbed two glasses, and poured, while Rhett stood several feet away just looking at me.

Suddenly, the room was so hot, the hair at the nape of my neck felt wet and sticky against my skin. I took a long swig. When I went for a second sip, Rhett caught my wrist.

"Parker, stop." He took the drink from me and set it on the counter.

"Don't say it." I swallowed the lump in my throat. "I feel so embarrassed for thinking that you might...you know. I mean, you're a Windsor. That was dumb of me. Um. Please forget I asked. I got caught up in the moment. And then Rowena put all these ideas in my head. And you're so good at pretending. This whole fake boyfriend thing really messed with my head. I should've known better. Literally the worst idea I've ever had. I—"

"Yes." His intense gaze pierced through my soul as he cradled my neck. "I'm in love with you. And not just since the last few days...or months. Parker, I've been in love with you for a very long time." He pressed his forehead to mine.

"What?" My mind went blank. "What?"

"I'm in love with you, Parker." His words sounded less strained than before.

"Why didn't you tell me?" I spoke into his lips. "We could've..."

"I don't know. I kept waiting for a sign, an opportunity. I don't know. I guess I was afraid you'd laugh in my face." He puffed out a breath.

"I'm not laughing." I gripped the lapel of his coat. "I love you too."

"You love me?" His eyebrows shot up slightly in surprise.

"I know. I'm shocked too." I slipped my hand under his coat. "Some time after you came back into town, I realized you and I could never be. I put my feelings for you in a box and threw it away."

"You can be so stubborn." He smiled, shaking his head.

"Me? I—"

He pressed his lips to mine. All logic went out the window right there and then. All I could think about was peeling layers of clothing off Rhett's body.

"Take it off." He pushed my coat off my shoulders.

I did as he asked and quickly removed my sweater, the t-shirt underneath, shoes and leggings. When I glanced up, I had about a second to admire Rhett's naked body before our mouths collided again in a desperate kiss.

By now, my body reacted to his every movement. When he bent down to grab me by the waist, my legs automatically wrapped around his. He did a full turn in place, before he asked, "Where's your bedroom?"

A rush of adrenaline exploded around my clit at the mere idea of having Rhett in my bedroom. But the thing was, I didn't want to wait that long to feel him inside me again.

"Too far." I tunneled my fingers through his hair and mumbled against his lips. "Couch."

He nodded and carried me the few steps from the kitchen to the living room. The cool upholstery against my back was a stark contrast to the heat emanating from his body and the hard as rock erection pressing into my entrance.

"I thought about you all day." He deepened our kiss, then moved down to suck on my taut nipple.

"I'm sorry I left this morning." I ran my hands over his muscled shoulders and back.

"Me too. We could've spent the entire morning in bed. Doing this." He gripped my butt cheek and swelled into me.

"Rhett." I moaned into his neck.

"I'm right here, Parker. I'm never letting you go." He plunged deeper into me as if he meant to leave his mark on me.

Our gazes locked. And I finally saw what had always been there, his silent I love you.

I cradled the side of his face as his hips settled into a fast and hard pace that hit my G-spot just right, over and over, until my walls tightened around his shaft. Oh, the man was magnificent. I wanted this feeling of pure contentment to last longer, but he felt too good. I tensed beneath him. My last ditch effort to contain the avalanche threatening to break through.

"Rhett." I met his thrust once.

He held me there, pulsating his want and desire into me. I held my breath, staring at him and waiting for the inevitable fall. He knew that if he moved even an inch, I would peak.

"I love seeing you come." With his gaze still locked on to mine, he pulled all the way out, rubbed his shaft all over my clit, then dove back in.

The minute I released my breath, the tiny flame rumbling over my clit exploded into the rest of me, followed by an all-consuming orgasm. Suddenly, the room was quiet and dark, and I was floating again. Somewhere in the distance, Rhett called for me right before he collapsed on top of me.

"Omigod." I hugged him to me. "It won't stop."

"Yeah?" He lazily moved his body to rock his cock inside me.

"Hmm." I moaned.

"Everything you do turns me on." He growled into the soft spot below my earlobe.

His erection filled me up again and rode me hard until I came a second time. Somehow, I went higher and fell even harder. It came in dense waves of pleasure that traveled up into my chest, and then, down to my toes. I pressed my lips to his pecs and reveled in the saltiness of his skin. Outside, the weather had dropped way below zero. But in here, our bodies were about to combust.

"What are you doing to me?" Rhett lay heavy on top of me, his face nestled between my breasts. "I only want you."

"It is possible you've ruined me for other men." I kissed the top of his head.

"Good." He took a handful of my breast and sucked on my nipple. "Because I can't stand it when other men touch you. Even when I know you don't want them."

"You make it sound like there are hundreds of men out there touching me every day." I pushed him off me, and he let go.

"For a long time." He sat on the middle cushion and pulled me in to straddle his lap. "It felt as though you loved everyone but me."

"I did go out of my way a lot to stay away from you, didn't I?" I glanced down at our sweaty bodies, and my nipples slightly brushing the light hair on his chest. "I think my body instinctively knew that if we ever touched..." I sighed. "I want you too much."

"I know the feeling. Hmm." He inhaled deeply, taking in my scent. His gaze dropped to his hand palming my breasts. He watched intently as if trying to memorize their shape and weight. "You are so beautiful." He cupped my face and pulled me in for a kiss. "I love you."

"I love you, too." My whole chest filled with euphoria. Saying those words to Rhett was as easy as breathing. "But now my leg is falling asleep."

"Hmm." He ran his hands up and down my thighs. "Okay." He lifted me and set me down on the cushion next to him.

I rolled off the couch and padded to the kitchen to put on my T-Shirt. He followed behind me and grabbed his boxer briefs. Looking that hot after sex should be illegal. I swallowed and reached for my wine and took a sip.

"I could get used to this." He drank from his glass.

"What's that?"

"You. Looking at me like I'm your last meal." He smirked and leaned in for a quick peck on my cheek.

I fake scoffed. "As if."

He chuckled, then pointed to the Christmas tree in the corner of the living room. "What's going on over there?"

"Oh." I puffed out a breath. "I started on it the day Dad fell. With everything that's been going on, I haven't had the time or motivation to finish."

"I can help you, if you want."

"You're on." I pointed at his chest. "But keep your shirt off."

"As you wish." He braced his hands on his hips. A move I'd seen him do a million times while clad in a three-piece suit. I had to admit, even without the fancy clothes, he looked just as striking. "Where do we start?"

"Okay. How about you group the berry and holly sprays in threes while I finish up the ribbons. Then we can hang the ornaments." I strode past him to get started.

"When we're done—" He walked up behind me and wrapped his arms around me. "—you're going to tell me what you were thinking just now."

"Just get to work." I pushed him toward the plastic totes filled with Christmas decorations.

To my surprise, Rhett knew what a spray and a pick were, and knew his way around a Christmas tree. He had mentioned before he used to help his mom decorate for Christmas when he lived at Windsor Mansion. But this was next level.

Seeing him here, happily helping me, made me realize that maybe he hated Christmas now because he missed the life he had when his mom and dad were still together. Was Christmas another thing he chose to stay away from out of loyalty to his mom?

"What do you think?" He stood back to admire his handiwork.

"I think it looks magical." I beamed at the glittering lights and big frosted ornaments.

"I agree." He reached for my waist and pulled me to him. "This was fun." He bent down and kissed me.

I melted into him. "Stay with me."

"Hmmm?" He stopped to survey my face.

"Spend the night."

"Okay." He bent down to kiss me again.

"Upstairs, last door on the right." I pointed to the stairs. "I'll be up in a minute. I need to lock up."

"I'll wait for you." He stepped aside and watched me as I flipped the latch on the front door, then turned off the lights.

Out of habit, I reached for my clothes and draped them over my arm. When I did, my phone fell out of my coat pocket. I glanced at it to make sure I hadn't missed any important messages and froze.

A message from Sofia was the last thing I had expected. The words flashed bright in the dimly lit room: "Can we talk?"

"Is everything okay?" Rhett asked.

"Yeah." I closed the messaging app. "The girls wanted to make sure I got home okay."

Why did I just lie?

"Let's go to bed." He offered me his hand.

I nodded and stepped into his embrace. Rhett loved me. Nothing could ever change what we had.

CHAPTER 17

Good morning, Mr. Mayor

Rhett

I picked up the strand of hair resting on my chest. Rubbing it between my index finger and thumb, I smiled at it thinking about all the times Parker sat in front of me at school, and it was all I could do not to reach out and touch the curl dangling a few inches from my desk.

By some literal Christmas miracle, Parker wanted me. In a matter of days, I had managed to go from the town's Scrooge to her fake boyfriend, and now the man she loved.

"Parker," I whispered her name and pushed her hair out of the way to look at her face, her rosy cheek and full lips. "I will never be sorry I waited for you."

Being with Parker was as easy as coming home. Though, as much as I wanted to stay in bed the rest of the day, I needed to go be mayor. The town was still recovering from the blizzard, and there were a million and one things to do at city hall. My chest filled up with actual joy when I remembered that Parker worked with me, that I didn't have to wait a full day to see her again.

"Good morning." Her eyes fluttered open as she stretched and tangled her body tighter around me.

"Good morning." I kissed the top of her head. "Nice Christmas bedding, by the way."

She chuckled. "Are you surprised?"

"Not at all." I hugged her tighter. "Very much on brand."

"Tell me we're taking the day off today." She groaned, kissing my chest.

"I wish. But there's a lot of work to do. I need to make sure the roads are clear. We need the tourists to come in and spend their money."

"Omigod. You're right." She sat up, pushing her hair away from her face. "The gingerbread house decorating contest is tomorrow." She made to leave the bed.

"What?" I grabbed her by the waist and pulled her to me. "I thought you canceled that."

"If by cancel, you mean postponed? Yes, yes, I did."

"Parker."

"Relax. We're making good money with Mrs. Birdwhistle's play." She peered up at me with doe eyes, then smiled.

"Don't look at me like that." I cupped her face. I wanted to give her the world every time she looked at me like I was her most favorite person in the world.

"I need to get in the shower. See you in the office?" She beamed at me.

"We're not done talking about this, Parker." Out of habit, I added, "We need to stay on budget."

"Absolutely." She gave me a quick kiss and climbed out of bed.

"Bah Humbug." I fell back on the pillows to watch her shapely ass as she strutted to the bathroom.

"I heard that." She called from the bathroom before she turned on the water.

I needed to get out of here before I decided to cancel my morning meetings and join Parker in the shower. Shaking my head, I let my legs fall over the side of the bed then rose to my feet. God, I loved waking up next to Parker.

By the time I got dressed and headed out, the sun had already peeked from behind the mountains. I made it all the way to Parker's front porch before I realized I had a huge grin on my face.

"Good morning, Mr. Mayor." Sam waved from across the street.

"Good morning." I waved and did my best to pretend I hadn't just been caught doing the proverbial walk of shame.

"Good morning, Mr. Mayor." Mrs. Birdwhistle turned the corner with her Shih Tzu in her arms. "Beautiful morning, isn't it?" She beamed.

"Yes, it is." I nodded and made a beeline to my car.

"Good morning, Mr. Mayor." Rowena appeared out of nowhere to join Sam and his pug.

Jesus, was everyone out walking their dog this morning? I waved, jumped into my car and drove. I suppose there was no sense in keeping our relationship a secret. The whole point of us fake dating was to make the town believe in the magic of Christmas. Somehow playing the boyfriend in love was easier before when my heart wasn't on the line. When Parker didn't know exactly how much power she had over me.

After a quick stop at my place to wash up and change my clothes, I decided to skip my morning coffee and go straight to the office. I swore the walk of shame continued as I crossed the bull pen to get to my office. Based on their looks and suppressed smiles, I was sure they all knew I spent the night at Parker's house.

So be it. I was in love with her. The sooner the town knew it, the better.

I sat behind my desk and took my first call of the day. The guys working on clearing the roads were making great time. With just a quick look out my window, I could see tourists crowding the Arabelle Square and all the shops. Parker had been right about that. People came here to experience the winter wonderland that was Winterstorm Village.

"Mr. Mayor?" Lila's voice came through the speakerphone. "Ms. Cruz would like to see you."

I rolled my eyes at her formality. No doubt that was Parker's idea to keep our relationship at work professional. I pressed the intercom button and leaned in. "Yes, Lila. She may come in."

A minute later, Parker sauntered into the room, looking like a goddess in a tight pencil skirt and a silky blouse. Her winter boots had already been replaced by leather pumps.

"Door open, closed?" Lila lingered by the threshold.

"Open." Parker blurted out.

"Ajar. Thank you." I sat back on my chair and waited until Lila waved goodbye with a big smile on her face. When we were finally alone, I rose to my feet and walked around my desk. "Is that for me?" I pointed at the cup of coffee in her hand.

"Yes. Sam mentioned you didn't stop by for your usual fix." The twinkle in her eye told me Sam had also mentioned he ran into me earlier today.

"They know I spent the night." I took the coffee and set it on the desk behind me as I pulled her toward me.

"Are you okay with that?" She ran her hand over my shoulders. "It's so weird how normal all this feels."

"I know." I cupped her face and captured her mouth.

Her body melted into mine as we both silently agreed to throw professionalism out the window. It was going to be a while before I figured out how to keep my hands off her. I deepened the kiss as I wrapped my arms tightly around her.

"I swear I had something work related I had to discuss with you." I pressed my face to her neck and inhaled her sweet perfume.

"Me too." She ran her hands up my chest and inside my suit jacket. "Okay. You first." She pulled away.

I leaned on the desk and grabbed hold of the edge to keep myself in check. "I sent you a copy of the updated Christmas budget."

"Rhett. No more cuts, please." She braced her hands on her hips.

"The Windsor family has decided to make a small donation to your cause. I figured it could pay for all those events you decided to postpone."

"Are you serious?" She covered her mouth. "How much?"

"Two hundred and fifty thousand." Seeing her face light up like a Christmas tree was worth way more than that amount.

"Omigod. Christmas is officially back on." She threw her arms around my neck and kissed me. "How did you get your aunt to fork over all that money?"

"She just wants to see this town succeed. You made an impression on her." I brushed the back of my fingers to her soft cheek. "You were right. People need Christmas. They need to believe in the magic of the season."

"You just made my day. I promise, we're going to make Gretchen so happy she donated all that money." She stopped for a breath, then beamed at me. "Now we have money to fix the clock tower. I mean, probably not in time for this Christmas. But, at least, we can start right away. The Arabelle Square looks so sad without it."

"It does."

"Ok. I have to go and tell the girls the good news. We have so much to do." She leaned in and kissed me on the lips before she turned on her heel and headed for the door. "Oh hey, Thor."

I glanced up and met Thor's grumpy gaze. I could only assume he had heard about the sizable Windsor donation. Jesus, was that how I normally looked like whenever Parker spoke of her grandiose Christmas plans?

As soon as the door shut, he stalked toward me. "There are much better ways to spend your trust fund than this? I hope you know that."

"I'm not sure what you mean." I touched my fingers to my lips where Parker kissed me.

"As Gretchen's lawyer, I know for a fact she doesn't care about your girlfriend's Christmas budget." Thor unbuttoned his suit jacket and stuffed his hands in his pockets.

"You sound like a Scrooge, Thor. Ease up." I walked around my desk and sat. "When were you going to tell me about your daughter."

"Not today." He stood taller. "We're still talking about you."

"Okay." I leaned back and smiled. Nothing could ruin today for me. "Hit me with it."

"You know what, it's good you're making use of your money, given how it's all going to go away come Christmas morning." He met my gaze.

"I'm well aware of the stipulations of my trust fund." I reached for the peppermint mocha Parker brought in for me and sipped. "If I don't marry Sofia, the money goes poof." I made an explosion gesture with my hand.

"This is serious, Rhett." He lowered himself down on the club chair across from me. "A breach of contract on your part will cost your family a fortune. The company may not recover."

"We've been through this, Thor. I made my choice. I'm with Parker. Whatever deal my grandfather and Dad made on my behalf when I was ten isn't my responsibility. It never was. I wasn't even a Windsor when he signed that contract."

"You think a technicality is going to fly with the king?" Thor met my gaze.

"I do actually. He wants his daughter Sofia to marry into a wealthy family. I'm not her way in."

We'd gone through this conversation a dozen times since he came into town. My answer hadn't changed. And now that Parker and I were together, hell would have to freeze over before I married someone else. A smile pulled at my lips. Marriage? Would Parker be open to the idea of marriage? To me?

"Jesus Christ. Look at your face." He pointed at me. "You're actually thinking about marrying Parker instead?"

"You're a mind reader now?"

"I don't need to be. Your face says it all."

"Thor, I appreciate your efforts to do right by Aunt Gretchen. But I'm with Parker now. I'm sure Sofia will find some other rich guy to bring to her dad."

"Your family stands to lose millions, Rhett."

"My grandfather should've thought about that. If he had, maybe Dad would still be here."

"You usually wait a lot longer before you make me feel like an asshole for even asking." Thor rose to his feet, fixing his gaze on me. "Tell me this wasn't the entirety of your plan?"

"What do you mean?"

"You come home to get the girl. You now have said girl. What happens now? You lose it all? Your family? The fortune? Then what? You're not even the elected mayor."

I clenched my jaw. "I'd like to believe that life is about more than just money."

"You were always quite the romantic." He clicked his teeth. "I'll let Gretchen know that your answer hasn't changed."

"I appreciate that." I stood to escort him out, but just then Lila barged into my office, looking like she had run up the stairs. I glanced at Thor then Lila. "Is everything okay?"

"Yeah." She fixed her skirt when she spotted Thor in the middle of the room. "Um. I mean yes. Your mom is here?"

"Are you asking me? Or telling me." I chuckled.

"It's okay, Lila." Mom strode in with her usual warm smile. "I just want to say hi to my son." She was dressed in a pant suit instead of her usual jeans and cable sweater, which could only mean one thing. She'd been to see Aunt Gretchen.

"Elise." Thor closed the space between them and hugged her. "It's good to see you."

"You too." Mom cupped his cheek. "Look at you. You're all grown up."

"Yeah, it's been a while since that happened." He winked at her. "I should go. I'm sure you two have a lot to catch up on."

I waited until we were alone to bring Mom into a bear hug. "I'm sorry I haven't called. The mayor had an accident."

"I heard." She gestured toward the bull pen. "My son the mayor. I'm so proud of you." She laced her arm through mine and ushered me to the seating area facing the fireplace. "It's been years since the last time I was here. But was that Parker Cruz sitting outside your office?"

"Yes."

The expectant and not surprised look on her face told me she already knew about Parker and me. Was that the reason she was here? She of all people should know what being with Parker meant to me.

"Why do I get the feeling you're here on Aunt Gretchen's behalf?"

"I'm sorry, Rhett. She called." She sat and brought me down with her. "To be honest, Rhett, I was flabbergasted when she told me you were the mayor of Winterstorm Village. I always assumed you came back to take over Windsor's media conglomerate." She said that last part with the usual flare that said she didn't care about Aunt Gretchen's empire.

"You know that's not why I came back."

"Parker." She patted my hand.

"Yes."

"Have you tried talking to her? Three years is not that long a time, Rhett." She cupped my cheek with so much love in her eyes. She truly believed me taking over the family business was the thing I wanted most.

"Are we really having this conversation? After everything you went through with Dad, you think me getting back into the fold is a good idea?" I furrowed my brows.

"This is different."

"How so?"

"You love it here. You love being a Windsor. Your father didn't. He was miserable here. He wanted California. Not this. But you." She let the idea linger in the air.

Yeah, I loved it here. My whole life was here. The time I had spent in California with Mom was the worst of my life. This was my home. And now I got to stay with Parker by my side.

"I do want to be here," I said.

"And I'm happy for you. I always regretted taking you away from here. I wanted you to have the choice your father never had." She sighed. "After talking to Gretchen this morning, I realize I never really said those words to you out loud."

"You want me to take the Windsor name back?"

"Of course, I do. That's your birthright. You're entitled to all of it. You're all Gretchen has left."

"You're starting to sound like her. Stop it. You're scaring me." I laughed.

She laughed too, taking my hands in hers. "Because she's right. And I was wrong to take you away."

"Why are you saying this to me now? You've only had, what? Eighteen years?"

"Because now you seem to be at a crossroads. I just want what's best for you. With your grandfather gone, things are different now. You no longer must choose between being free and being a Windsor." She leaned in to hug me. "I'm only here because I want you to be happy. Do you believe me?"

"I do, Mom. Thank you for saying that." I hugged her back. "I'm with Parker now and I'm happy. If I marry anyone at all, it would be her."

It's always been her.

I gave Mom a quick kiss on the cheek and rose to my feet. "How about we get dinner tonight so I can properly introduce you to my girlfriend?"

Mom had come here to say her peace because after all this time she still felt like she owed Aunt Gretchen something. But now that she had delivered her message, she relaxed her stance.

"I told Gretchen you were the only person who was more stubborn than Rhett Windsor, Senior. You're most certainly you're grandfather's grandson. The good parts, anyway." She sighed as she studied my features, looking for the truth. "I'm so happy Parker finally saw how amazing you are. What took her so long?" She shook her head.

"Wait until you meet her. Meet her again, I guess." I ambled back to my desk and pressed the intercom button. "Lila, could you see if Parker is available?"

"She just left. She said she had an important lunch meeting. Should I call her?"

I checked my watch. It was way too early for lunch. "No, don't worry about it. I'll talk to her later."

"A mysterious lunch date." Mom raised her eyebrows. "Be careful, Rhett. When it comes to her family, Gretchen won't let anything get in her way. She always gets wants she wants."

Seeing Mom standing in the middle of my office, I thought of Thor's visit and Parker's odd behavior last night after she read a text message on her phone. If I didn't know any better, I'd say Aunt Gretchen was planning something. Mom was wrong in thinking I was the only one who could be more stubborn than my grandfather.

That title belonged to Aunt Gretchen, the queen of stubbornness. She was not going to stop until she got exactly what she wanted, until she made me fulfill that ridiculous marriage contract with Sofia.

Parker, don't fall for Aunt Gretchen's antics.

CHAPTER 18

If You Can Stand It, So Can I

PARKER

No idea why I fled the office as if I had something to hide. Yeah, seeing Elise Parker spooked me. I didn't need to be a rocket scientist to know that she was in town because somehow, she found out Rhett and I were together now. The question was, did she come to wish us well or to bring Rhett back to California?

Either way, I couldn't worry about her right this moment. I slowed down my pace as soon as the Chalet Pastry shop came into view on the corner of main street. Through the tall windows, I spotted Rowena and Sam wiping down tables and carrying dirty dishes behind the counter.

When Sofia texted earlier asking to see me, I figured meeting her at my friends' coffee shop was the best place for it. But now, I wasn't so sure. I had a feeling that whatever Sofia wanted to talk to me about, it would involve tears. She had lost Rhett for good. Marriage contract or not, Rhett was mine.

The wind blew and picked up flurries of snow. Some of

them kissed my face while others clung to my heavy coat. Behind me, the Arabelle Square filled the air with Christmas music and happy chatter. I smiled at the picturesque scene. Somehow, Rhett and I had gotten the holiday spirit back on track. Dad would be proud that instead of fighting, we were getting along like he'd asked. Well, we were doing way more than getting along.

My core heated at the memory of Rhett in my bed this morning. The man had no right to look so freaking hot at the crack of dawn.

"Parker." Sofia waved at me from across the street.

"Hey." I smiled, ignoring the odd dread that settled in the pit of my stomach.

Why did I agree to talk to her? Oh right. Guilt was a bitch. If there was a way for me to make Sofia less sad about losing Rhett, I wanted to at least try.

"Let's get inside." I motioned toward the coffee shop.

I pushed the door open, and let Sofia in. As soon as she had her back to me, I gestured to Sam and Rowena to fix their stunned faces.

"Hey. Have you two met Sofia?" I leaned on the counter. Sam nodded, but I continued with the introduction. If they remembered her, it was because we were gossiping about her yesterday morning. "Sofia, these are my friends, Rowena and Sam."

"Hi, it's so good to meet you both." She shook their hands in a way that seemed so regal.

"Nice to meet you too." Rowena said in a too bubbly voice.

I shook my head once, and she recovered quickly. "You have to try our blueberry muffins. I just baked a new batch. Why don't you sit down, and I'll bring you a plate?"

"Great idea." I took Sofia by the hand and pulled her toward the table by the front window. "Sorry about that. My friends are a little too excited to meet royalty."

"Oh. That's okay." She lowered herself to the chair and waited for me to do the same. "You're probably wondering why I wanted to see you so urgently."

"Honestly? Yes." I chuckled nervously. "What's going on?"

"I can't believe I'm doing this." She ran a hand through her blonde hair as her gaze searched the small coffee shop for answers that weren't there.

"Gretchen sent you, didn't she?"

"Yes."

"You want to just blurt it out? Rip it off like a Band-Aid?"

"I need to marry Rhett. Up until you showed up, he had said he would marry me. My family is really counting on this merger to go through." She said it all in one breath. "I'm not saying you should give him up forever. It's just for a little while. Three years to be exact."

Three years was a long time to be married to someone. I surveyed Sofia's soft features, her bright blue eyes and overall fairy-tale princess vibe she had going on. The dread in my stomach turned to something darker that I could only describe as jealousy. If Rhett spent any amount of time with Sofia, I had no doubt he would fall in love with her.

"So, you think you can marry Rhett and then let him go after three years?" I furrowed my brows. "Have you met him?"

She blushed. "I get what you mean. But I'm willing to stand by the terms of the contract. Three years is all I get."

"I have to admit, this whole arranged marriage sounded less crazy when we were back at the mansion, with carolers strolling through the ballroom dressed in 19th century frocks."

I rubbed the side of my face. "But out here in the real world—"
I pointed at Sam behind the counter as proof of my reality. "—
it sounds crazy."

"That's funny." She offered me a bright smile. "I can see
why he loves you."

"I love him too," I confessed.

"I know. It's why Gretchen says you'll do the right thing."
She swallowed. "The contract expires on my twenty-fifth
birthday, that's in two weeks on Christmas day."

"That's why you came into town."

"It's now or never, I suppose." She chuckled. "Rhett wants
to be a Windsor again. He told me that a year ago."

The idea that not so long ago Sofia was Rhett's confidant of
sorts made me see red. Before I could stop it, I saw the two of
them in my mind's eye. I saw them kissing and touching.

"Parker?" Sofia reached across the table. "Are you okay?"

"Yeah."

"I know it sounds hard. But it's also simple. We all get
what we want. Just not at the same time."

"You can't ask me to give him up." I met her gaze with tears
in my eyes.

"I'm only asking that you don't stand in the way of what he
really wants. He wants his family. His home. His name. He
wants it all back." She bit her bottom lip. She knew her words
cut me deep, but she pressed on. "Their company will lose
millions. He'll lose his trust fund. Don't let him throw it all
away."

"I'm not doing this." Tears streamed down my cheeks. "He
wants to be with me."

"There was a time when he wanted to be with me too. He
was willing to try." The corner of her lips pulled up as if she

were recalling some bittersweet moment. "My first year in college—"

"I don't need the details." I wiped my cheek. "Is there anything else Gretchen wanted me to know?"

"I'm sorry, Parker." She squeezed my hand. "My family needs me to do this."

"Yeah, you're in a really tough spot here." I pursed my lips.

"I should go." She made to get up. When I didn't stop her, she cleared her throat and rose to her feet. "Thank you for meeting me."

I lifted my gaze just as she strode out the door. I stared at her retreating form until the falling snow hid her from view. What the hell was I supposed to do with this? Jealousy didn't begin to cover how I felt. I sure as hell didn't want Rhett spending any amount of time with Sofia, let alone three years.

But at the same time, I knew for a fact Sofia was right about Rhett wanting to be a Windsor again. I saw it in his eyes the night of the party. He was at home in the mansion. He fit in that space. Who was I to stand in the way of what he really wanted?

"That was heavy? I can't believe she looked you in the eye and said all that with a straight face." Sam placed a muffin in front of me.

I glanced up at him. "You were eavesdropping?"

"We both were." He pointed at Rowena as she set a hot chocolate next to my pastry.

"What are you going to do? You can't just give up Rhett like that. He loves you. You guys waited so long to get here. It hasn't even been a week." She plopped herself down on the chair next to mine.

"I'd say screw it." Sam sat across from me. "They can't make him marry her."

"That's the thing." My gaze flicked from Sam to Rowena. "He wants to."

"You don't know that." Sam pointed a finger at me. "Sofia might look like an angel, but that doesn't mean she's one. She's lying. Even if she's telling the truth. College was a long time ago. At least for Rhett." He shrugged.

"Oh no." Rowena stared at me with eyebrows raised. "I know that look. You're actually thinking about letting him go."

"No. I love him." I wiped my cheek with the back of my hand. "I can't stand the thought of him marrying someone else."

As if I had wished for Rhett to come and make it all go away, his beautiful face appeared on the other side of the window. He shook his head once, then made for the door.

"We'll be in the kitchen." Rowena shot to her feet and grabbed Sam by the hand. "Hi, Rhett." She waved at him. "Bye, Rhett."

"Hi." Rhett offered me a tentative smile before he sat next to me.

"Hi." My chest tightened as my mind conjured all kinds of scenarios where Rhett spent the rest of his life away from here, away from me. "What are you doing here?"

"Looking for you." He adjusted his weight. "Mom came to see me."

"Oh. Why? I thought she never wanted to come here."

"Aunt Gretchen called her. She's determined to—"

"Get you to do the right thing?" I interrupted.

"She got to you too?" His gaze darkened. "Parker, we don't

have to do anything we don't want to do. I hope you know that."

"I do. And that's the whole point. I mean, Sofia made a lot of good points. The main one being that you, at some point, wanted to be married to her."

"Jesus Christ." He pinched the bridge of his nose. "I was twenty-two, fresh out of college. An arranged marriage felt like the path of least resistance. I tried. I really tried. But she's not who I want."

"Don't say it."

"I want you. It's always been you, Parker."

"What about your family? Are you ready to lose them? To lose the Windsor fortune?"

The more I said the words out loud, the more they made sense. Even if his eyes showed how much he loved me. I knew that over time, he would resent me for making him choose between his family and us. I never really met Rhett's parents. But from the few times I saw them, they seemed in love.

So what made them get a divorce just a short time later? What made his mom move cross-country and change his last name? I didn't want that for us. Ending things now was the most logical thing to do.

"I don't want to end up like your parents." My eyes widened in surprise because I hadn't realized how much I agreed with those words. How afraid I was to have Rhett hate me for real. "I can't do this."

"Parker, you can't compare us to my parents. I want to be here with you. There's nothing for me in California." He reached for my hand.

His warmth rushed up my arm and eased the fears brewing in my chest. Rhett completed me. I was one hundred percent addicted to his raw energy and the way he made me feel. I never wanted to look into those soulful eyes and not see love.

"With time, you will grow to resent me for taking you away from your family." I inhaled his scent and tightened my grip on his fingers. "You have to do what's right."

"Parker." He wiped my cheek gently. "Don't do this. We can work thorough anything. You and me."

The plea in his voice cut me. But I couldn't make Sofia's words go away. They rung true in my head. He stood to lose so much. I'd always known Rhett wasn't for me. After he came back after being gone all middle school, I knew he could never be mine. That was the reason I built a wall between us. I was so stupid for letting it come down.

"We should've stuck to our contract," I said quietly.

"What contract?"

I glanced over my shoulder to Sam and Rowena. Of course, they were eavesdropping. I was okay with that. But this next part, they could never know about.

I leaned in and whispered, "To fake date until the town believed in the magic of Christmas again."

Yeah, the more I said that, the more I realized how naive I'd been. Had I come up with that whole crazy plan because I wanted a reason to get close to Rhett? A tiny voice in my head murmured yes, but I brushed it away. How we got started didn't matter? What mattered was that we couldn't keep our relationship going.

"But now we're telling the whole town that it didn't work out?" He let go of my hand and sat back, crossing his arms over his chest. "That won't confuse them?"

Why did that move look so hot on him?

"I don't know. I mean, everyone's happy. They love the idea of us."

"I know." His tone was clipped. "What do you want from me, Parker? Hmm?"

"Would it be too much if I asked you to stick to the plan?" I asked tentatively. Because even now, I could feel the kind and loving Rhett floating away from me, only to be replaced by the cold and intolerant Rhett. I could see his wall of ice coming up again, shutting me out like before. I didn't realize it would hurt so much. "It's only until Christmas. Isn't that when you have to get married and save your family from ruin."

"My family doesn't need saving." He let out a dark laugh that shook me to my core. I knew enough about Rhett now to see he was hurting, but he would never show it. "You really think you can keep this charade going for two more weeks?" He cocked an eyebrow, looking deeply into my eyes. After what felt like several minutes, he added, "Fine. If you can stand it. So can I."

"Oh." I didn't think he'd agree so quickly. Not that it mattered. Whether he fought for us or not, the result would be the same. We were never meant for each other. This cosmic attraction between us was no more than sexual desire. It didn't mean anything. "Right. So we're on the same page then."

"Seems we are. I should've known you'd leave too." He pushed his chair back. "I need to get back to the office."

"Rhett." I reached for his hand but stopped midway.

Rhett Parker, soon-to-be Rhett Windsor again, wasn't mine. Not anymore. What the hell just happened? I sat there and watched him walk out the door and sauntered across the town square back to city hall.

"Rhett. I'm sorry," I mumbled.

"Are you okay, girl?" Rowena pulled up a chair. "Did you guys break up?"

"I don't know. I think so." I turned to look at her blurry face as tears pelted down my face. "I guess we're fake dating now?"

"What?" Sam dropped what he was doing behind the coffee bar to join us.

He took the chair on the other side of me while I stared at the empty seat across from me. I swore I could still pick up Rhett's scent in the air.

"I didn't think the town would be okay with us breaking up so soon, you know?" I pushed the hair away from my face, trying to piece together the bits and pieces of our conversation.

Did we really break up?

"Who asks to wait until Christmas day to break up?" Rowena took my blueberry muffin and bit into it.

"Who asks to fake date?" Sam asked, shaking his head.

"Apparently, I do. He's supposed to marry Sofia by Christmas."

"Oh girl." Sam stood and hugged me. "Everyone wins except you."

I was officially fake, fake dating the love of my life.

CHAPTER 19

Holy Hot Santa

Parker

True to his word, Rhett did exactly as I'd had asked. In front of the townspeople, he was the caring boyfriend who loved Christmas again. But when we were alone, he was back to his old grumpy self. Two whole days had gone by, and it still hurt like hell to be outside of his sphere.

But Christmas was almost here, and we had lost so much time with the snowstorm, we had to focus and make sure all winter events happened as planned.

"Hey, sweetie." Sam winked at me from behind the counter. "I'm working on your coffee right n..." He froze as his gaze cut to the front door.

"Good morning, Sam." Rhett's icy tone made the temperature in the coffee shop drop to way below freezing.

"Good morning, Mr. Mayor." Sam offered him a weird smile then tried to make eye contact with me.

I simply shrugged as if I didn't care that Rhett was in the room. As Rhett had pointed out yesterday, we didn't need to pretend to be friends when we were alone. Sam and Rowena knew every detail of the arrangement. So at least, I didn't have to pretend that I was happy with our current situation. And why was he even mad at me? He was the one who agreed to marry someone else years ago. Not me.

"Peppermint mocha?" Sam offered.

"No thanks. Just a black coffee. I'm in a hurry." He stood behind me.

I inhaled deeply, then my heart sank when I couldn't catch his woodsy scent. In the morning, he always smelled like his verbena and lemon grass bodywash. I hated that I knew that now.

"Soooo, Parker." Sam squeezed a good measure of chocolate syrup into a cup before placing it under the espresso spout. "How are the festivities coming along now that the snow has been cleared out and the town is bustling with tourists. It's so good to see how your vision has come to life so magically."

"Are you okay?" I furrowed my brows at him. I had specifically asked all my friends not to be weird about all this. Especially not in front of Rhett.

"Sorry." He mouthed.

I shot a quick look over my shoulder. "Everything is awesome." I winced because I was sure I had sounded like the guy from the Lego movie. "That reminds me. We made a few adjustments to the gingerbread house decorating contest."

"Oh yeah? What's going on? What do you need?" Sam asked, as his gaze flicked to Rhett.

I had this conversation with Mrs. Birdwhistle yesterday. All day I waited for the right time to ask Rhett for a favor. But he was just impossible to talk to these days.

Behind me, Rhett made a growly sound as he leaned over and grabbed his coffee. "Thanks, Sam." He waited another moment for Sam to enter the amount on his screen, then paid with his iWatch.

I stood there basking in his scent.

In the next two breaths, Rhett strode out of the coffee shop and the room swayed into focus once again. "This is a disaster."

"What? No. You're doing great." Sam placed my peppermint mocha in front of me. "I thought that went great. Did you like how I threw some props your way?"

"Yeah, very subtle. Thank you." I sipped from my cup. "So, for real now, we didn't want to cancel cookies with Santa day, so we're combining it with the gingerbread house decorating contest this weekend. Is that okay? I think that'll bring in a bigger crowd."

"I think that's a great idea. We'll set up some tables outside with heaters and hot chocolate. It's going to be great." He beamed at me.

"Thank you. Thank you." I leaned in and kissed his cheek. "I'll see you this afternoon so we can finalize our plans."

On the way to city hall, Mrs. Dankworth and Mrs. Birdwhistle caught up to me. "Parker, dear." Mrs. Birdwhistle smiled politely. "Good morning."

"Good morning." I did my best to keep my smile on. I knew what she was going to ask, and I wasn't ready to tell her there was no way in hell I could deliver on what she wanted. "How are you ladies today?"

"Great. Did you ask him?" She got straight to the point.

"Um. Yes, and no?"

"What do you mean?" Mrs. Dankworth asked. "We won't

take no for an answer. Our new mayor must be this year's Santa. The kids love him."

"Right." I picked up the pace. If I could make it to city hall, I'd be safe. "I'm on my way to ask him right now."

"That's wonderful." Mrs. Birdwhistle beamed. "We'll come with you. I need measurements for his costume."

Rhett was going to hate me for putting him in this situation. But in my defense, I suggested him for this year's Santa when he was being a total Scrooge about the holidays. I had to admit, picturing Rhett in a fat Santa suit made me smile.

"You know what? I think that's a great idea. Let's go ask him right now."

Emboldened by Mrs. Dankworth and Mrs. Birdwhistle support, I marched up the stairs to the top floor and didn't even stop by Lila's desk to see if Mr. Mayor could see us. With my heart thrashing in my ears, I knocked on Rhett's office door.

"Come in." His deep voice sent butterflies to my belly.

"Go on, dear." Mrs. Dankworth egged me on.

"Right." I shook my head to clear my thoughts and entered.

"Yes?" Rhett glanced up, then down, then up again. "Parker?"

"We—" I started to say, but Mrs. Birdwhistle beat me to it.

"We need your measurements for your Santa suit." She used her teacher's voice, which meant she wasn't taking no for an answer.

"Why do I need a Santa suit?" Rhett glanced at me for a beat.

"Cookies with Santa tomorrow night," I interjected. "Remember? I told you about it last night. At my house. Over dinner. That we had together." God, I sounded like Sam now.

"Right. Dinner." Rhett sat back in his chair. "What do you need me to do?" he addressed the two women.

"It's an easy job. You just need to sit and get your picture taken with the kids. We'll have cookies and hot chocolate for them."

"Sounds like a fun time. Anything else?" He smiled politely.

"I just need your measurements to tailor the Santa suit we have." She motioned for him to come to her.

I pressed my lips together to stifle a laugh. But this right here was priceless. I stood there as Rhett slowly rose to his feet and ambled toward the two women eager to get their hands on him. He let them measure his waist and shoulders and then his inseam. The whole time he shot daggers at me.

"He's going to be the best Santa. Isn't he ladies?" I asked.

He shook his head at me. For a split second, I was sure he was suppressing a smile. But then the moment was gone. God, I missed him.

"You're all set, Mr. Mayor." Mrs. Birdwhistle wrote on her small notebook, then turned to me. "I will see you tonight at the coffee shop to talk about setup and decorations."

"Yes, of course. Sam and Rowena are excited to be hosting." I walked them out before Rhett had a chance to change his mind. And just because I could never help myself when it came to Rhett, I poked my head back in and added. "See you tonight, babe."

"Later, Sugar cakes," he replied.

❄

"He's not here." I announced to Rowena who was in the process of supervising the gingerbread house decorating contest. "I really don't want to gaslight kids into thinking they just missed Santa. You know I can't stand to let Mrs. Birdwhistle down."

"She's not your teacher anymore." Rowena rolled her eyes. "Here, hold this." She shoved a big tub of frosting into my hand. "I need to get more gummies."

I stood awkwardly in place until Joe raised his hand and asked for more frosting. "Oh yeah." I ambled to him and served a big dollop on his tray. "Omigod. You have a real talent for decorating. Look at you."

"The kids were helping me." He shrugged. "How are you and Mr. Mayor doing? Are you happy?"

"Very happy." I offered him a smile that showed all my teeth. "He's a great guy."

At some point in the next week, I needed to start telling people that I didn't think it was going to work between us. I glanced down at my watch. Rhett's wedding was literally in ten days. We had to figure out a way to tell people that it was over.

"Yeah, great guy." Joe lifted his chin toward the street.

When I turned around, my jaw dropped. Rhett joined the group of kids outside wearing a red suit. Not a fat Santa suit, but a red velvet suit that hugged his biceps and pecs in all the right places.

"Holy hot Santa." I pressed a hand to my forehead.

What was Mrs. Birdwhistle playing at?

"Parker." Sam waved at me as he zigzagged his way through the crowded coffee shop.

"I see him." I pulled Sam toward the wall, away from Joe's prying ears.

"Don't make eye contact. You might get pregnant." He made to cover my face.

"I know." I slapped his hand out of the way. "I mean. Pfft. I don't care. He's just a guy in a suit."

"Who's great with kids and put on a red suit for a noble cause." Sam did a double take when I gave him the stink eye. "What? Are we back to hating him?"

"Nooo." I extended the o into three syllables.

"Parker." Mrs. Dankworth joined us. "Isn't it wonderful? So many people came out. It's all so festive."

"Yes." I smiled at the twinkling lights and all the happy faces around the room. "It's perfect."

This Christmas was just perfect.

"I'm in charge of pictures. Come with me. We need one of you with Santa."

I let Mrs. Dankworth drag me out of the store to where Rhett sat in his big Santa chair, looking more lickable than he should. I slowed my pace as I approached him. I wasn't sure how to play the girl in love while at the same time not letting him see how much I still wanted him.

To my surprise, Rhett didn't skip a bit. He flashed me a blinding smile, then offered me his hand. "Would you like a picture with Santa?"

Omigod.

"Yeah sure." I took his hand and sat on his lap.

How easy would it be to melt into him and run my fingers through his hair, maybe kiss his lips and forget this whole wedding fiasco he had waiting at home.

"Thanks for doing this, by the way." I adjusted my weight.

He released a breath slowly. "We're here to save Christmas, right?"

"Yeah."

"Say, cookies with Santa." Mrs. Dankworth said in a cheery voice before snapping a few photos. "These look great. Thank you. Who's next?"

In the back of my mind, I knew I had to get up and let the next kid have a turn, but for the life of me, I just couldn't move. If my heart was not beating so hard against my ribs, I would've thought time had stopped. If he tried to kiss me right now, I was sure I would throw myself at him. I had to get out of here before I scarred the children for life.

When I made to get up, his hand on my hip tightened and effectively sucked all the air from my lungs.

"Rhett." I didn't have more words for him because I honestly didn't know what I was asking of him...

Kiss me, please.

Don't let me go.

Let me go before I change my mind.

Stay.

Don't marry her.

"I need to go inside and judge the contest." I stole a quick glance at his lips before I meet his gaze again.

"Yeah, you gotta go." He gripped my elbows and set me on the asphalt.

I gave him an awkward wave and headed back inside where the air was easier to breathe.

The rest of the night I focused on the contest and my responsibilities as a judge. Toward the end, when it was time for participants to present their gingerbread houses, Rhett came inside to help one of the kids finish up her house.

When the final tally came in, Joe was announced the winner. "Congratulations, Joe." I hugged him and presented him with his gold medal that had the Chalet Bakery shop logo on it.

"Thanks." He kissed his medal.

"Congratulations." Rhett pressed his body to my side before he wrapped his hand around my waist. "That was a bad ass gingerbread house. The kids didn't stand a chance."

"Not that it matters, but I'm donating my prize money to the Clock Tower restoration fund." Joe glared at Rhett.

"Everyone wins." I pulled Rhett toward the door.

This was so not the time to be playing the jealous boyfriend. I wanted to tell him that I wasn't his anymore. But his hand on my waist was putting all kinds of bad ideas in my head. His body felt so good, somehow hard and inviting at the same time.

I glanced up and got lost in his intense gaze. This was also so not the time for him to do his smoldering thing.

He leaned in a few inches. "Can we talk in private?"

"Sure." I pointed up the street, where a few scattered flurries danced in the air. "What's up?" I gathered my coat around me.

"I just." He cleared his throat. "I didn't want you to hear this from anyone else. I started the process to change my name back to Windsor." He puffed out a breath, smiling at the ground. "Aunt Gretchen had a judge on standby to sign the petition. Anyway, the court order should come through in a day or so." He took a step away from me.

"Wow. Congratulations. You're a proper Windsor again." I swallowed the lump in my stomach. "Good luck with all that." I turned to leave, but then both our phones started ringing.

I fished my phone out of my coat pocket to look at the screen, and he did the same.

"It's the hospital," he said as he answered. "This is Rhett."

I snapped out of it and tapped on the answer button. "This is Parker."

"Parker. It's Dr. Chen. I know you're busy with the gingerbread house decorating contest, but I wanted to call and give you the good news myself."

"Is Dad, okay?"

"Yes, he's great. He's demanding that I send him home tonight." She laughed. "I told him I'm waiting on one more blood test. If everything comes back clean, he should be able to go home tonight. Just in time for Christmas."

"Omigod. That's the best news. Thank you so much for calling. Can I see him right now?" I asked as I turned to face Rhett who was now off his phone and looking at me with genuine concern.

"Of course. That's why I called." Dr. Chen laughed.

"I'll be there in a few. Thank you." I hung up, then faced Rhett. "I gotta go. Bye."

"He's going home." He stepped toward me.

"Yeah. I'm going there now to wait for his tests results." I buttoned my coat and started walking.

The hospital was a mile away. A long walk was exactly what I needed to clear my head and forget about that fact that Rhett was one step closer to being married.

"Let me drive you." He wrapped his hand around my elbow to make me turn around.

"No, thank you." I gestured toward the shop. "I don't need you."

I turned on my heel and winced. I hadn't meant for the "I don't need you" part to come out sounding so resentful. We were grown adults who had decided not to be in love.

"It's starting to snow, Parker." He fell into step next to me. "Don't put yourself in danger just to spite me."

"What?" I stopped in my tracks. "You think this is about you? Don't flatter yourself. I rarely think of you these days." I spun again and picked up the pace.

I made it to the end of the street before I heard Rhett call me stubborn. He let out a big sigh that made me think he'd given up on playing my knight in shining armor. In the next beat, he stalked past me then cut me off to open the door to his Tesla. "Get in the car, Parker."

"I don't want you there."

"And that's fine by me." He gripped my elbow. "But your dad wants to see me. So. Get in. Now."

I was too stunned to argue anymore, so I let him put me in the seat and buckle me in. Why did Dad want to see him? Oh crap. Did he know about us? Oh no. How was I going to tell Dad that Rhett and I only had a quick fling that didn't mean anything. How could I ever lie to him? Even if I tried, Dad would see the truth in my eyes.

"What do you think he wants?" I asked as soon as Rhett climbed in behind the wheel.

"Maybe he wants to make sure we haven't killed each other yet." He raised a brow, put the car in drive, then peeled off the curb.

"What are we going to tell him? We can't tell him about the whole fake dating thing, right?" I shifted my weight to face him, which was a mistake. His cut jaw and proud nose made me want things I couldn't have. "We agreed."

"We tell him the truth, Parker." He fixed his gaze on the road.

Even if I wanted to tell Dad the truth. I had no clue what that was anymore.

CHAPTER 20
Don't Make Me Wait

PARKER

"Why didn't you wear the fat Santa suit?" I asked to steer the conversation into a different direction. I hated that Rhett seemed so indifferent about our situation. As if we hadn't experienced the most life-changing two weeks of our lives. "Mrs. Birdwhistle worked all night to get the alterations finished for today."

"I had this suit that fit me better. I had it made for a friend's Christmas party." His gaze cut to me for a beat. "In Cancun."

If Dad had not had his accident two weeks ago, Rhett would be in Cancun right now, possibly playing hot Santa with some super model from New York City.

"Nice. Does Sofia know about this girlfriend of yours throwing parties by the beach?" My stomach twisted at the idea of Rhett spending any amount of beach time with another woman.

"Sofia is not in charge of my social calendar," he said dryly.

I blinked to clear my vision. What I really wanted to ask was if he was really getting married in a few days' time. He was a Windsor again. And now he needed to do what his family expected him to do for the good of the company.

I couldn't decide what was worse. Rhett serial dating supermodels or Rhett settling down with someone like Sofia. The images of him in Cancun quickly inundated my mind. And just because I was really feeling sorry for myself, I pictured him in a bathing suit with some hot model having sex by the ocean. I glanced down at my fisted hand.

"Are you mad at me for not wearing the fat suit? Or because I had travel plans before your dad's accident?" Rhett's voice cut through my dark reverie.

"I don't care what you do with your time." I shrugged.

We drove in silence the rest of the way. As soon as he pulled into a parking spot, I bolted. I wanted to see Dad and get my life back to normal. Back to when I didn't have all these feelings for Rhett.

I rushed to the elevator bay and pressed the call button several times. When the elevator doors slid open, Dr. Chen greeted me with a pleasant smile.

"Parker. You got here fast." Dr. Chen put her hand out to stop the doors from closing. "Mr. Mayor. Good to see you." She beamed at Rhett over my head.

"Good to see you too, Dr. Chen. Please, just call me Rhett." He side-stepped me and joined Dr. Chen. "Are you coming?" he asked me.

"I'll ride up with you two." Dr. Chen waved me in. "Tony is doing great. You'll see."

"Has he been discharged yet?" I stepped inside the elevator car, keeping my back to Rhett.

"Not yet. I'm working on it." Dr. Chen squeezed my shoulder. "He's doing great. You don't need to worry."

"How soon would he be able to return to work?" Rhett asked.

"That's up to him. All I ask is that he doesn't overdo it. Rest is the best medicine for him right now."

As soon as the doors opened, I headed to Dad's room. For no reason at all, I started crying the moment I found him sitting up in his bed eating dinner like he hadn't just spent two weeks in and out of consciousness.

"Dad." I darted to him and hugged him. "You look great."

"I feel great." He patted my hand. "I guess all I needed was a good nap." His gaze flicked to Rhett. "Rhett, thank you for coming to see me."

"I'm glad you're doing better, Tony." Rhett ambled to the foot of the bed. "Dr. Chen says you're ready to come back to work."

"I'm ready." Dad nodded.

"There's no rush, Dad. We have it all under control." I took his empty cup and filled it with water. "We've had the best holiday season." I inhaled a breath. "Rhett has done a great job as mayor."

"I heard." Dad offered Rhett a nod of approval. "I had no doubt you'd do an exemplary job. Didn't I tell you, Sugarplum? That he was the best man for the job?"

"Yeah, Dad. You did."

Dad's gaze bounced between Rhett and me twice before he furrowed his brows. I shifted my weight to avoid eye contact with him. Last week, I would've been ecstatic to tell him about me and Rhett. But now, I didn't know where to begin. Rhett wanted to tell Dad the truth. But what was the point? Rhett wasn't mine.

"Is everything okay with you two?" Dad pushed his tray out of the way and sat up a little higher on the bed. "I'm glad to see you're getting along. But you seem sad, Sugarplum."

I opened my mouth to tell him I wasn't sad, but the words didn't come out. How could I tell him that I wasn't sad? That what I was, was extremely jealous. And maybe angry that even though Rhett was in love with me, he couldn't choose me.

"I'm in love with your daughter," Rhett said calmly as if he was merely commenting on the weather, and not confessing to my own dad.

"I know." Dad smiled.

"What?" I squinted my eyes at him.

"Your daughter loves me too," Rhett continued.

"No, I don't." I glared at Rhett.

"I know that too." Dad released a breath.

"Wait. What? Since when?" I turned to face him.

"Since always, Sugarplum. I'm just glad you two finally figured it out." He patted my hand on his shoulder.

"Well, don't be so glad, Dad. Rhett is marrying someone else."

There. Rhett wanted to tell the truth. There it was.

"Oh dear."

"Which is why." Rhett paused for a beat. "I'm tendering my resignation effective immediately as mayor and your deputy mayor."

"What?" My gaze cut to him. "You can't quit."

"I have to, Parker." He released a breath. "Our mayor is back. He can take it from here. My position was always meant to be temporary."

"I see." Dad offered Rhett a kind smile. "Is there anything I can say to make you stay?"

"I'm afraid not." Rhett stepped back from the bed and stuffed his hands in the pockets of his trousers. "It was an honor working with you, Tony."

I stood there as Rhett and Dad said their goodbyes. After tonight, I was never going to see Rhett again. Not being with him hurt, but at least seeing him at work every day helped eased some of that pain. I blinked away tears. When I glanced up, Rhett was gone.

"Dad, why did you let him go?"

"The man has to follow his own path, Sugarplum."

"No." I shook my head.

Before I realized what I was doing, I found myself running down the hospital corridor, chasing after Rhett. I was wrong to let him go. He knew that.

"Rhett." I stopped just a few feet from the elevator bay. "Don't marry her. I was wrong. I was wrong about everything."

"No, you weren't." Slowly, one tentative step after another, he closed the space between us and cupped my face.

My eyes fluttered closed. The warmth of his hand traveled from my cheek all the way down to my toes. I placed my palm on his chest, wishing I could do more. I wanted to feel his lips on mine again, to wake up in his arms every day for the rest of my life.

"Rhett."

"It took losing you to finally get my head out of the sand." He bent down and brushed his lips to mine. "I can't ask you to wait for me. You deserve so much more."

"Then don't make me wait."

Choose me. I wanted to scream those two words at him.

But what would be the point? He had already made up his mind. Or rather, his aunt had already decided for him. And he wasn't fighting back. There was only one path for him.

"I spent years wishing you were mine. Wishing this contract with Sofia's family would go away. Wishing I could be a Windsor and not break Mom's heart. Just wishing. And doing nothing about it." He slid the pad of his thumb over my lips. "Until you came along."

The love I found in his eyes broke my heart. His feelings for me didn't matter. It was why he never told me how he felt about me. Why he spent his days fighting me on anything and everything. Because he knew that was the only kind of interaction we could have.

I pushed him to want something he knew he couldn't have.

"I made this worse for you. Didn't I?" I took in his scent one last time.

"I'm trying to do the right thing here, Parker. I'm sorry." He surveyed my face as if he wanted to memorize my features.

"Okay." I made to turn away and leave.

But then, he grabbed me by the elbow and pulled me to him. He allowed me three full seconds to refuse him before he bent down and captured my mouth in a desperate kiss.

I tunneled my fingers through his soft hair as I tasted all of him, sucking on his velvet tongue as if my life depended on it. I let him back me into an empty room and cage me against a wall with his body.

The heat emanating from his skin clung to me as a rush of desire engulfed me. This chemistry we had was like black magic. It made me forget why we had even said goodbye before. As he ran his hands over my butt and pinned me tighter with his hips, I considered the very real option of waiting for him.

I dug my fingers into the straining muscles of his shoulders, deepening the kiss. I wanted this man in a way that scared the hell out of me. He moved down to kiss my neck and my breasts. I didn't care that we were in a hospital. Or that anyone could barge in on us at any moment. Feeling his cock inside me was all I cared about in this moment that was possibly our last.

That single thought washed over me like a bucket of ice water. And then Gretchen's words echoed in my head. "There are worse things than being the duke's mistress." I saw Sofia clearly in my head, with her innocent doe eyes, utterly in love with her future husband. I saw a life filled with stolen kisses and clandestine meetings.

I couldn't do that to myself. I couldn't do that to her. We couldn't do that to her.

"Parker." He pulled away first as if he could read my thoughts. "Jesus." He panted a breath on my lips. "You drive me absolutely crazy. That's why I can't stay."

"Yeah." I let my arms drop to my sides. "You gotta go."

"Parker, I swear—"

I pressed my index finger to his mouth. "Don't make promises you can't keep. Just go."

He nodded once. I glanced away and waited until the door opened and fell shut to let my tears flow.

Sometime after sunset when the hospital room darkened, I decided feeling sorry for myself wasn't helping. No doubt Dad was wondering where I'd gone. I picked myself off the floor and wiped both cheeks. With a sigh, I opened the door and walked into the brightly lit corridor.

Two steps in, the elevator dinged, and Sofia's angry voice

broke the silence. I glanced behind me. When I confirmed I was alone, I ducked back into my previous hiding room, leaving the door cracked open. After everything that happened with Rhett earlier, I just couldn't face Sofia's angelic disposition.

What was she doing at the hospital?

"I'm getting married and that's final." She rushed down the corridor.

A man chased after her, gripped her arm, then caged her with his body. "What happened, princess? A taste of the real world got you scared?"

"I'm not afraid."

"Then prove it." He pulled her in and kissed her.

By the way she dug her nails into his back, I could only assume this wasn't their first kiss.

Omigod. Omigod. Omigod.

I covered my mouth to stifle any sound. What the hell was happening? Sweet Sofia had a lover? What happened to being madly in love with Rhett? I rummaged through the pockets of my coat looking for my phone. When I couldn't find it, I searched the room. Sure enough, at some point while I was making out with Rhett, the device had dropped out of my pocket and landed near the bed.

A loud thud against the door got my attention. I tiptoed to it and slowly pushed on it so it wouldn't fly open under their weight. Wincing, I threw the lock and stepped back.

"Bennett, stop. Please." Sofia panted a breath.

Keeping an eye on the door, I dropped to my knees and grabbed my phone to snap a photo of them. Not that Sofia was doing anything wrong. It seemed her arranged marriage to

Rhett was an open one. She allowed Rhett to see other people. So why shouldn't she do the same?

Me: Guys, I'm at the hospital. Sofia is here making out.

Sam: Whaaaat? Who is it?

Me: no idea.

Rowena: picssss

Briar: no way. I thought her wedding was in a few days.

What? A few days? Rhett didn't mention that. I stared at Briar's text. She was very close with Ava Walton. Of course she had the scoop on the impending Windsor wedding. It hurt to think about Rhett saying "I do" to someone else. Even if it wasn't forever. It still felt like I had lost him.

Sam: hello? You can't drop a bomb on us and then disappear

Briar: I'm sorry, P

Rowena: pics??

Me: one sec.

The kissing on the other side of the door stopped. Sofia mumbled something I couldn't quite make out, then she took off running.

"Fuck," Bennett said through gritted teeth, then slammed the wall.

When footsteps fell in rapid succession, I opened the door just in time to see him take the stairs. Was he going after her? I darted to the stairwell and managed to catch them kissing again. They were so consumed by their kiss; they didn't even notice when I took a picture.

The minute I sent it to the group chat, Briar replied inside of five seconds.

Briar: OMG that's Bennett Windsor. The black sheep of the family. Rhett's cousin!!!!

Me: OMIGOD

Me: OMIGOD

Sam: I'm on my way.

Rowena: same

Ten minutes later, Sam, Rowena and Briar practically burst out of the elevator car. I stuck my head out the door and waved them over.

"Guys, in here." I stepped back to let them in.

"Okay, tell us what happened?" Sam shut the door and turned to me expectantly.

"Rhett and I came to see Dad."

"Oh, sweetie." Rowena beamed at me.

"No. Not like that. We're still broken up." I released a breath. "After he left, Sofia showed up with Bennett. I really didn't see his face. The picture is kind of blurry. But she called him Bennett."

"I'm sure it's him." Briar brought up the picture on her phone and zoomed in. "Here, let me find a good picture of him. He has a huge social media following. All he does is party." She took a minute to scroll through her socials, then showed us her screen. "That's him."

"Oh, sweet baby Jesus." Sam took the device from Briar. "He's hot. That's some good Windsor genes."

"Let me see." I snatched the phone from Sam.

Yeah, Bennett was a younger, less grumpy version of Rhett. From the sound of it, he was really into Sofia. I smiled at his picture as I recalled their conversation.

"I got the sense that he didn't want Sofia to marry Rhett," I said.

"So what are you going to do?" Rowena grabbed the phone

from me. "You have to tell Rhett. He's about to marry someone who's in love with his cousin."

"It's an arranged marriage. I don't think love is part of the equation." I ran a hand through my hair.

Even if I knew that Rhett wouldn't care if Sofia was sneaking around with his cousin, for a moment, I thought maybe Bennett could stop the wedding somehow. But the truth was, only Gretchen and Sofia's parents could do that.

"There's nothing he can do," I said.

"I'd say send Rhett the picture anyway. Just so he knows." Briar shrugged.

"Is the wedding really happening next week?" I asked Briar.

"Yeah, the ceremony's taking place at the mansion. Ava invited me." She winced and hugged me. "But I'm not going. The house is full of dignitaries from Sofia's country. Too stuffy for my taste."

"I think you should go." Sam braced his hands on his hips. "And unmask that little minx."

"We're not doing that." I chuckled. "Technically, she's not doing anything wrong. Rhett's been doing the same, dating whoever he wants."

"So that's it?" Rowena put her arm around me. "You're letting him go."

"What else can I do? Did I tell you Gretchen offered me money to break up with Rhett?"

"Oh wow." Rowena's eyebrows went up in surprise. "You didn't tell us that."

"Yeah." I nodded once. "She even donated two-hundred-and-fifty thousand dollars to the city's Christmas fund. I think she feels guilty."

"Are you sure it was her?" Briar asked. "Gretchen doesn't seem like the type who does guilt."

Sam and Rowena shrugged, with their eyes full of pity.

I ambled to the hospital bed and plopped myself down. Both Rhett and Sofia were going into a marriage neither of them wanted. Today, Sofia showed a new side of her. She was passionate and stubborn as all heck. She'd come to see me to ask me to let Rhett go, even when she herself was struggling with letting Bennett go.

"I'm sorry, Parker. My family needs me to do this." Her words echoed in my head.

Why did her family need her to marry Rhett? Was it something as cliché as her family being on the brink of ruin, and so, they needed the Windsor money? Whatever it was, the end result was the same. She was determined to follow through on what her family expected of her. Bennett or no Bennett.

CHAPTER 21
I Broke Parker's Heart

Rhett

"We need construction to resume immediately. You know what? Get Steve on the line. I'll talk to him." I glanced up to find Thor leaning on the doorframe to the library. "Yeah, call me back when you get him."

"I see you've already taken over for Gretchen." Thor pushed off the door and ambled over to sit across from me. "The Windsor desk suits you."

I scoffed. "It's a work in progress."

"Well, here's more progress." He dumped a manila folder in front of me. "Court order has been issued. You're officially a Windsor again."

"Thank you." I glared at the folder.

No idea why I thought there would be a drastic change in the air once I was officially back in the fold. I felt the same. No matter how long I carried the Parker last name, I supposed I never fully stopped being a Windsor. Now that it was all said and done, I was glad to be part of my family's legacy again.

If only I hadn't had to choose between my family and Parker. I was such an asshole for letting her go. But too much was at stake. And she was right. As much as I hated to compare myself to Dad, I was already feeling resentful for not being allowed to come back on my own terms. These days, I couldn't stand to be in the same room as Aunt Gretchen or Sofia.

None of this was their fault, and yet, here I was being the grumpy asshole.

"You're welcome." Thor let out a breath. "I already delivered the good news to Gretchen. The wedding can go on as scheduled." He paused and leaned forward. "Three years will go by in a flash."

"Maybe." I sat back on my chair. "But I can't discount the fact that Parker could fall in love with someone else in a day."

"If she loves you—"

"I would never ask her to wait for me. It's disgusting. I couldn't even promise her that I would try and get out of this ridiculous contract." I picked the pile of papers to my left. "I've gone through every clause. I don't see a way out."

"I did the same. It's iron clad. You can't walk out without leaving your family in ruin." He pursed his lips. "I'm sorry I couldn't be any help."

"It's not on you."

"Well, you're busy. I'll let you get back to work." He rose to his feet. "Let's do drinks tonight."

"I'm not in the mood for company." I rubbed the creases on my forehead. "Some other day."

"As you wish. Call me if you need anything." He nodded once and left.

I glared at the contract pages and began reading for the hundredth time. Three years living under the same roof as

Sofia. Once a child was produced—their words, not mine—Sofia and I would have the option to get a divorce before the end of the three years, provided both families agreed. While we were both allowed to have lovers on the side, the first year required absolute fidelity.

This particular clause had been added by Aunt Gretchen. She wanted to be sure that Sofia had my child and not some random stranger's kid. If Sofia cheated after the wedding, the contract would be null and void. I scoffed. If only I would be so lucky to have Sofia be tempted by someone else.

But sweet Sofia would never do something like that, which was why I had agreed to forgo the pregnancy test mandated by the contract. It was demeaning to her. It was bad enough she was tethering her life to someone who didn't love her. Even after a divorce, our lives would be forever linked through our child.

My insides twisted with remorse every time I saw her. While I thought of no one else but Parker, Sofia didn't waste time showing me how much she was looking forward to our wedding. And how much she loved me. She wanted this marriage to work. Meanwhile, I was counting the days until I could be free of her.

I stopped reading the long list of clauses as my brain flooded with a lot of stupid ideas. The loudest one being that there was nothing stopping me from going over to Parker's house right now and spending the night with her.

I touched my fingertips to my lips. How long before I stopped thinking about her and our last kiss?

"You should see the garden." Mom beamed at me as she took the seat Thor had just vacated. "It's so beautiful. Gretchen is practically building a wedding venue out there.

Your nuptials are going to be the most talked about event of the year."

"I didn't think you cared about that kind of nonsense." I met her gaze.

"I do when it's my son's wedding." She glanced at me with pity in her eyes. "I'm sorry things didn't work out the way you wanted. At least this way, Parker gets to walk away with her heart intact."

"I doubt she would agree." I gestured toward the gardens, hoping to change the subject. "I can't believe how fast Aunt Gretchen put this shindig together."

"Do you really think she started planning all this just last week?" She raised an eyebrow.

"Of course not." I let out a breath.

I didn't blame Mom for taking Aunt Gretchen's side on this one. In her mind, Mom was convinced her and Dad's love story was happening all over again. She wanted to spare me the heartache. Dad loved her. He never stopped loving her. But Mom simply couldn't love the man Dad became when he was under Grandad's thumb. Dad and he had a complicated relationship to say the least. Mainly because Grandad expected everyone in his household to do as they were told.

Mom showed Grandad that money couldn't buy everything. It was why she'd moved us to California and moved heaven and earth to change my last name to Parker. She wanted me to have the choice Dad never had. She believed that this way Parker and I would have a shot at trying again someday in the future. Assuming Parker didn't find someone else in the next year or so.

I fisted my hand at the thought of her with any other man. I saw red every time the intrusive thought invaded my mind.

"Oh Rhett." Mom reached across the desk to squeeze my hand. "I'm so sorry. I'm sorry I couldn't do more for you."

"It's not your fault." The phone rang and saved me from having to sit here and tell Mom I was okay with this whole bullshit wedding. "I have to take this. It's work."

"Yeah. Sure. Go ahead. Gretchen tells me you're a natural at it. You've been back for only a week and you're already making progress." She beamed at me.

"I'll see you later, Mom."

I spent the rest of the afternoon going from one fire to the next. The holiday season was the money maker for our media conglomerate. We couldn't afford mistakes or even a slow day.

After my last meeting, I allowed myself to look out the window to check in on the preparations for the so-called wedding of the year. Mom was right. The garden looked magical. Parker would've loved to have seen it. The whole winter wonderland aesthetic was her thing.

I chuckled to myself just thinking about her Christmas budget and her passion for bringing the best holiday season to the town and our visitors. Shaking my head to stop myself from going down my usual Parker rabbit hole, I focused on the tree-line beyond the wedding venue. There, in the distance, a mop of blonde hair caught my attention.

Was that Sofia? What was she doing so far away, at the edge of the property? I moved in closer and squinted at the woman running at full speed to make sure it was really her.

For no reason at all, I got that sense that something was wrong with her. People didn't run like that just because. Something happened to her. I grabbed my heavy coat off the sofa facing the fireplace and headed out to check in on her. Nightfall was less than a half hour away. It wasn't safe to be that far off from the main house.

I had a clear vision of her being chased by a bobcat or some other animal, too frightened to know the difference between a scared woman and a hunter.

I followed the garden path past the crew of people working diligently under the white tent. I hadn't been out here since the last time I brought Parker out here to show her the clock tower. That night I'd used Aunt Gretchen's watchful eye as an excuse to kiss her again. I should've known then that getting so close to her would break both our hearts.

I picked up the pace and made it to the edge of the property in under ten minutes. But when I got to the spot where I'd seen Sofia, she was gone. The snow back here wasn't as well kept as the areas closer to the main house. But it was easy to see which way she'd gone after she left the beaten path.

"Bennett, I'm scared." Her voice traveled as if it'd bounced against the thick tree trunks. The wind blew quietly and carried her soft cry. "What am I going to do? Say something."

The cold seeped through my leather shoes, but I stayed frozen in place. Bennett and Sofia? I blinked to focus on the two bodies entangled with each other as if they were lovers. Lovers?

"How is this possible?"

"You're not seriously asking." She shoved him away from her. "I'm pregnant, Bennett. What are we going to do?"

I had heard enough. I pushed off the tree and let them see me. Up until I started fake dating, and then dating, I never considered myself the jealous type. Even now, seeing Sofia with Bennett, I felt nothing. But here was the thing, I was tired of Bennett's antics. He just didn't give a fuck about anything,

With his face in my clear line of sight, I stalked toward him, grabbed him by the lapel of his heavy coat and punched him in the face. "What the fuck did you do?"

"Rhett, let him go." Sofia grabbed my arm. "Please."

"What did I do?" Bennett recovered from his shock of seeing me and shoved me away from him. "Get off your high horse. It's not like you care about her. You barely acknowledge she exists."

"This is not about me." I pushed back. "You got my fiancée pregnant, you fucking asshole."

"I didn't," he blurted out, then winced. "I mean. I did."

I punched him again. This time, he was ready for the blow. He stumbled backward, but didn't make an effort to retaliate. Good. For once in his life, Bennett Windsor was admitting that he had crossed the line.

"Rhett. Don't hurt him." Sofia stepped in front of me. "Please."

She meant to block Bennett from view, except she barely reached my shoulder. I could still see my cousin's pompous face. He was admitting guilt, but not exactly backing down.

My gaze flicked to Sofia. "You don't get to ask for anything. You don't get to say please with tears in your eyes. I broke Parker's heart to do right by you."

"I'm so sorry." She placed her hand on my chest. "It won't happen again. I promise."

"What won't happen again? You fucking my cousin under my roof?" I glared at her. "How long has this been going on?"

Not that it mattered. The real issue here was that she was pregnant. Not that she was having sex with my cousin.

"Don't answer that," Bennett said through gritted teeth as if he was the offended one here.

"What?" I turned to him. "This isn't a court of law. You're not her lawyer."

"Seems to me she's going to need one," he said through gritted teeth.

Bennett had gone too far this time. Anger bubbled in my chest at the implication of what they had done. I let my whole body rise and fall with every breath while indignation coursed through me. And then the most basic truth hit me—Sofia was pregnant.

The contract didn't require her to be a virgin. But she at least needed to show up not pregnant to our wedding night. I met her gaze as my exasperation lifted.

"Don't say it." Tears streamed down her cheeks. "Please. Don't say it. I swear, I'll do anything you ask." She paused for a moment. "I'll never see him again. Or speak to him. Whatever you say. I'll do it. Please. Please."

"Our contract is null and void, Sofia. I won't marry you."

"You have to, please." She threw her arms around my waist. "My father will kill me."

I glared at Bennett. "You should've thought about that before you slept with him. He doesn't care about anyone but himself."

"The all-mighty Rhett Windsor the third has spoken." He put his arms out as he sauntered toward me. "What should be our punishment?"

"Bennett." Sofia turned to face him. "Stop it. You're making it worse."

"What is there to make worse?" He took her hand and pulled her toward him. "At least now you won't have to carry on with this ridiculous farce of a wedding contract."

"My family can't afford to forfeit the contract, Bennett." Sofia placed a hand over her forehead.

The pain in her eyes cut me. She wasn't the first woman to fall prey to my cousin's indefinable allure. But she was, for certain, the first one to be absolutely ruined by him. What a fucking asshole? He knew what was at stake and he seduced her anyway. Why would he do this?

"I'm sorry, Sofia." I offered her a weak smile. "I can't help you."

I turned toward the beaten path and headed back to the house. The whole way, I considered the crazy turn of events. I was free of my contract with Sofia's family. But what would Parker think if she knew that I threw Sofia to the wolves and just walked away?

Since I agreed to marry Sofia, I had taken the time to investigate her family's business and their financials. They were at the brink of bankruptcy, which was why they were in a big hurry to marry into the Windsor wealth. Aunt Gretchen was more than happy to help them in exchange for a royal title. I couldn't help but wonder if this whole arrangement was just a whim on her and Grandad's part. The Windsors had it all... except a royal title.

It wasn't as if the child wasn't a Windsor. I couldn't just send her away because the situation suited my ulterior motive. I wanted to be with Parker. But I didn't want anything to tarnish my love for her.

I had to do the right thing.

CHAPTER 22

Some Kind of Christmas Miracle

RHETT

By the time I reached the main house, my annoyance with Bennett had subsided. The cold air brushed my cheeks as a plan to help Sofia gelled in my head. If Parker were here, she would already have a very elaborate scheme to make sure Sofia got what she wanted.

"Rhett," Sofia called after me. She was several feet behind me, with Bennett on her heels. "Let's talk about this."

I ignored her pleas, mainly because I didn't want to have this conversation in front of the crew building our wedding venue. In the corner of my eye, I spotted Mark making a beeline to the stone steps that led to Aunt Gretchen's wing. Though the terms were clear on the matter, the decision to call off the wedding wasn't entirely mine. So it was good that Mark was getting ahead of the situation.

"Stop." Sofia cut in front of me. "We need to talk. Before you call my parents, let me explain."

"Fine. Explain away." I gestured toward the open door to

the library. When Bennett made to join her, I blocked him. "I need to speak to Sofia alone."

"Fuck off." He stepped closer to her.

"Don't test me, Bennett." I glared at him. "I'm the only one who can help her."

He pressed his lips together. The dark storm brewing in his eyes was the only sign that he didn't agree with my methods. I didn't give a shit what he approved or didn't approve of. Maybe he'd forgotten about all his previous escapades. But I hadn't. The last time I found him in a similar situation, he jumped out a window and left me to deal with the mess he had created.

I entered the library and shut the door behind me. As soon as I did, Sofia turned on her heel and started talking fast. "I promise it was just the one time. It didn't mean anything. It won't happen again."

"It didn't mean anything?" I chuckled and gestured toward the door. "Are you sure? Bennett is out there ready to burn down the place just because you're in here with me."

"My parents will never forgive me." She flopped herself down on the sofa and settled her gaze on the roaring fire in front of her. "Don't be mad at me. I just wanted to feel," she mumbled mostly to herself.

That sounded like the cold hard truth.

"I'm not mad at you, Sofia." I strode around the sofa and sat on the club chair adjacent to her. "Just give me a minute to think."

Her eyes snapped up at me. "You're going to help me."

"How far along are you?"

"Six weeks."

"So you met before coming here?" I braced my arms on my thighs.

She nodded, releasing a breath. I felt like such an asshole. My violent reaction to her news was not what she needed. She seemed so alone and afraid.

"Jesus." I squeezed her shoulder. "I didn't mean to scare you out there."

My gesture prompted her to scoot over and hug me. "You're the only who can save me." She pressed her cheek to my chest. "Don't tell anyone."

"Was that your plan? To marry me and pretend your baby was mine?" I asked. I wasn't even mad at her plan. "Was that why you were trying to get me to sleep with you?"

"Yes." She hugged me tighter as if I was her only lifeline.

I suppose I was. Now that Bennett was off the hook so to speak, he would leave her to deal with the consequences on her own. "Do you love him?"

"It didn't mean anything." She shook her head.

"I can't help you if you're not honest with me." I cocked my head to look at her.

"I do love him." She lifted her head to meet my eyes. "I don't know how it happened. For as long as I can remember, all I wanted was to be your wife. To be in love with you. My feelings shifted, and I didn't even notice." Her whole body relaxed as if a big weight had been lifted off her shoulders.

"And my cousin?" I asked. "Does he feel the same way?"

Her eyes watered. "I don't know."

In the next beat, the sound of a heavy boot against a massive wooden door echoed in the library. The doors bust open, and Bennett barged in looking like a wild animal. His dark gaze zeroed in on me and Sofia. "Get off her." He practically growled the words.

"Or you'll what?" I shot to my feet. "Punch me for talking to *my* fiancée?"

His jaw flexed. "She's not yours. She's pregnant with my baby."

"Boys." Aunt Gretchen strolled into the room. "Enough. The entire crew outside can hear your thundering voices."

"Then you already know what happened. What he did?" I pointed at Bennett, feeling like we had gone back in time fifteen years when we spent a lot of our time in this mansion fighting over everything and anything. "He slept with my fiancée."

Aunt Gretchen winced and put up her hand. "I heard. No need to repeat it." She turned to Sofia. "Is it true? About the baby?" She gestured in Bennett's general direction.

"Yes. I'm so sorry." Sofia shook her head. "I have no idea how it happened. I mean...I'm sorry."

"No more apologies." Aunt Gretchen put up her hand then turned to meet my gaze. "You read the contract?"

"I did," I answered.

"Then you're aware that by her admittance, it is now null and void?" She cut a glance toward Bennett.

"I know." I nodded once.

"What are you going to do?" she asked. "We will need to notify her parents."

"Rhett." Sofia bit her lip.

Aunt Gretchen was a shrewd woman. As I suspected, she had already done the math and had decided the end justified the means. She wanted a royal heir, and now she had one.

"She's carrying a Windsor. We can make it work." She offered me a kind smile.

"The hell you are." Bennett stepped in. "Aunt Gretchen, you can't make her marry him. I get that he's your favorite. But she doesn't want him. She wants..."

"Yes?" I asked when his voice trailed off. "She wants... you?"

"Yes." He braced his hands on his hips. "She wants me. And I want her."

Sofia's eyebrows shot up in surprise. Her gaze cut from Bennett to me then back to Bennett before she spoke. "Are you sure?"

"Of course I'm sure." He furrowed his brows as he stepped toward her.

"One second, Bennett." Aunt Gretchen put out her arm and stopped him in his tracks. "What are you saying? Are you willing to take responsibility for what you did?"

God, she was good. Aunt Gretchen didn't care who of us married Sofia. And by the small wrinkle that formed in the corner of her eyes, she was ecstatic that Bennett was finally stepping up to do the right thing. Had my cousin finally met his match? I glanced at Sofia, who had stopped breathing, waiting for his answer.

"That's exactly what I'm saying." He glanced up as if he couldn't believe what he was about to say next. "I want to marry her."

"Well, I don't know." Aunt Gretchen turned her back to Bennett to beam at me. "What do you think Rhett? Are you okay with all this?"

My mother was right. Aunt Gretchen always got what she wanted.

"If Sofia agrees. Then yes." I faced Sofia. "He can be an insufferable ass. Are you sure he's the one you want?"

Tears pelted down her cheeks as she met his gaze. Bennett placed his hands behind him and stepped closer. A move I'd seen him do a million times before with other women. Though, somehow, this time he seemed sincere, in love. "I'd like to be more than a bodyguard to you. If you'll have me."

"I do. I really do." She practically floated into his waiting arms.

"All's well that ends well, don't you think?" Aunt Gretchen hooked her arm through my elbow. "By some kind of Christmas miracle your cousin is finally settling down."

"If I didn't know any better, I'd say—"

"You'd say that you're finally free to pursue anyone you want. I wonder how much groveling you'll need to do to get Parker back." She patted my hand. "I have a few ideas, if you want."

"I think you've done enough." I wrapped my arm around her. "Thank you."

"For what? I didn't do anything. You should thank your cousin." She pointed at the happy couple.

"Not a chance." I shook my head and chuckled.

THE NEXT MORNING, I arrived at the Chalet Pastry shop as soon as they opened. I had hoped to see Parker before she went to work, but as soon as I entered the shop, Mrs. Birdwhistle cornered me.

"You're going to need a big gesture to win Parker back.

The poor girl." She shook her head at me. "And Bennett? The boy is shameless. He always was."

Seriously? How in the world did she know about Bennett and Sofia already?

"Of course we're still happy for you. You and Parker were meant to be together. Of course, we all thought you had worked out your marriage contract *before* you approached Parker and—"

"Mrs. Birdwhistle, I have to go. I'm late to my meeting." I headed for the door.

"Just so you know. If you ever decide to run for mayor, you have our vote," she called out.

"I appreciate that."

Out of habit, I took the route from the coffee shop to city hall. I was really going to miss being mayor. Who knew, maybe now that Bennett had decided to settle down, he might be interested in taking over as CEO.

"Rhett." Rowena darted across the street to catch up to me. "Were you looking for Parker?"

"Yes, I was going to check city hall."

"She's at home." She pursed her lips. "She hasn't left her place in days. I came over last night, but she doesn't want to see anyone."

If I were in Parker's shoes, sitting at home, thinking she was marrying someone else, I would be devastated. I hated that I was the one who made her feel this sad and broken-hearted. I had to fix it.

"I have to see her." I blew out a breath. "Thanks for letting me know."

"Yeah, no worries. Hey." She gestured toward Mrs.

Dankworth's flower shop. "I wouldn't show up empty-handed."

"Great idea. Thanks." I headed straight for Mrs. Dankworth's shop.

As soon as I crossed the street, I spotted her peeking out her window. But when she saw me coming, she stepped away from it. Given how her friend Mrs. Birdwhistle knew the whole story already, I could only assume Mrs. Dankworth knew as well.

I'd be lying if I didn't admit this was one of the reasons why I never told Parker how I really felt about her. Failing in this town was like failing on a big stage. But now, it seemed, I had made things much worse. I managed to avoid being the guy who got dumped by the town's sweetheart. Instead, I was now the asshole who broke her heart.

I pushed the door open to the small shop. When the bell overhead chimed, Mrs. Dankworth stopped watering her plants and turned to face me. "Good morning, Mr. Mayor," she said dryly.

"Good morning." I cleared my throat. Mrs. Dankworth was obviously not happy with me. I stepped toward the counter. "I'm not the mayor anymore."

"Oh, that's right. My mistake." She waved her hand in dismissal then continued watering her plants.

"I would like to buy some roses," I said tentatively.

"Oh." She spun around so fast; she knocked off one of her potted pansies. I made to help her clean it up, but she shooed me away. "Leave it. Are the roses for Parker?"

"Yes." I smiled at her. "I need something that says—"

"That you were wrong. And hardheaded?"

"Okay." I rubbed the creases on my forehead. "Also, that I'm sorry. That I want to spend the rest of my life with her."

"Oh." Her eyes watered. "Of course." She scurried toward the back of the store and came back with a floral arrangement that was like the one she'd made for my first fake date with Parker. "I knew you couldn't marry that girl, Sofia. Especially during Christmas. And after that winter storm."

"Right." I fished my wallet from the inside pocket of my heavy coat and handed her my credit card. "Thank you."

She quickly finished the transaction and sent me on my way. When the door closed behind me, I glanced back in time to see her pick up her phone. I had no doubt she was calling her entire book club to let them know I was on my way to grovel.

I considered driving the half mile to Parker's house. I didn't want the whole town to see me carrying the huge bouquet of roses. But I needed time to really think about what I wanted to say to her. And maybe it was time I stopped worrying about Parker rejecting me. I had a long road ahead of me. Because Parker Cruz was nothing if not the most stubborn woman I'd ever met.

Ten minutes later, I stood at Parker's front porch. I knocked on the door and stepped back. After a minute, I tried again. And again. And again. "Parker, I know you're home. I can hear 'Jingle Bells' playing." I set the flowers down on the doormat. "Can we please talk?" I braced both hands on the doorframe, then shot a glance behind me. Sure enough, Sam was once again walking his pug. He beamed at me and gave me two thumbs up. I waved at him then faced the closed door again. "I didn't get married. It's a long story."

The footsteps on the other side of the door made my heart

race with anticipation. A week without Parker had been pure torture. The deadbolt disengaged with a satisfying snap and the door swung open.

My smile faded the minute I saw Parker's dad crowding the threshold. "Good morning, Tony."

"Good morning, Rhett." He stood there and waited for me to say something else.

"I would like to speak to Parker. Is she available?"

"Tell him I'm not home," she shouted from the kitchen.

Tony winced, then blew out a breath. "I'm sorry. My daughter is not home."

"Right." I picked up the flowers. "When will she be back?"

"I'm not sure." He shook his head.

"Tell him I'll be available to him when hell freezes over." Parker turned the volume up.

"My daughter will—"

"I heard her." I put up my hand. "Can you make sure she gets these?" I handed him the roses. "Can you tell her I didn't get married."

I glanced down and exhaled. Every time I said those words out loud, I realized what a jerk I had been. From the beginning, I knew I had a marriage contract hanging over my head. I knew I couldn't give Parker what she deserved. But I was too selfish to stay away. Since the first time we kissed, I should've known that playing this fake dating game was only going to end with her getting hurt.

"I'll make sure she gets your message." He nodded once. When I turned to leave, he called after me. "Rhett."

"Yeah?"

"Give her time. She's still processing everything that happened. And..." he pursed his lips. "She's hurting."

"I am so sorry. I never meant for her to get hurt."

"I know. You'll figure it out." He stepped back and shut the door.

Figure what out?

I stood there staring at Parker's red door, while "All I want for Christmas" played on the other side. Her whole house smelled of roasted chestnuts and baked cookies.

How was I ever going to get her back? I stopped on her stoop and looked for Sam across the street. Maybe he had some advice to give me on how to get Parker to talk to me. But he was gone.

The whole way back to Windsor mansion, I played our whole relationship in my head. At first, I agreed to her crazy plan to pretend we were dating because I liked the idea of sharing a secret with Parker. I should've known that getting close to her would rekindle all the feelings I'd had for her since we were kids. Especially after I came back from California.

In the time I was away, my feelings for her went from a childhood crush to something more, something that felt like love. But she hated me then. Or as she put it, she hated that pompous version of me. I latched on to her rejection because loving her from a distance was safer.

"Rhett." Abigail beamed at me from the front door as soon as I pulled into the graveled driveway. The moment she realized I was alone, her smile faded. "What happened?" she asked when I climbed out of the car.

"She doesn't want to see me." I raked both hands through my hair.

"Oh, Rhett. I'm so sorry."

"I never should've asked her to be my girlfriend. It was so

selfish of me." I shook my head. "I should've married Sofia first then came back once I was a free man."

"You know that would've made a lot of people very unhappy." She cupped my face. "Don't give up on her. She loves you. I saw it the day I met her."

"I broke her heart."

"Tell her that." She patted my chest.

"What? That I know I hurt her? She knows." I headed toward the front door. I needed a stiff drink to get me through the rest of the day.

"No." Abigail followed me inside the house. "Tell her everything you feel. Since the beginning." She flashed me a knowing smile. "Show her your letters."

"I don't know what you're talking about," I lied.

"She needs to know how much you have loved her and for how long." She wrapped her arms around my waist and squeezed me tight. "I'll go make you some tea, while you think about it."

Show her?

Ripping my heart out of my chest and leaving it on her stoop would be easier than showing Parker those letters. I couldn't do that.

CHAPTER 23

All The Letters I Never Sent

"This is easily one of the best pot roasts you've ever made." Dad sat at the kitchen counter happily eating his dinner.

"Thanks, Dad." I pushed around a carrot in my bowl. "How was your first day back at work."

"It was great. Rhett left everything in perfect order. He's a natural."

"Yeah." I pushed my food away from me.

Hearing his name and how perfect he was made feel nauseous. I was sure that was a defense mechanism of sorts. If I didn't feel this debilitating anger toward him, I would've ran out to see him when he stopped by this morning.

Dad clicked his teeth. "Oh, Sugarplum. I'm sorry, so sorry he hurt you."

"It was my fault. I never should've let him get so close." I lifted my head to meet his eyes. "I was right to hate him this whole time."

"I don't want to defend him."

"Then don't."

Dad let out a breath. "I'm only saying this because I know you want to be with him. He's free to choose now, and he wants to be with you." When I didn't say anything, he continued, "I looked at the city's financials this afternoon. The big donation we received from the Windsors? That came from Rhett's personal account."

"Okay. So the guy has more money than he knows what to do with. What does that have to do with me?" I shrugged, ignoring the very real possibility that Rhett donated that money because I wanted a bigger Christmas tree for our town.

"It was designated to compliment your Christmas budget." Dad raised an eyebrow. "He obviously did it for you. To make you happy."

"He did it to ease his guilt for stringing me along." I scoffed.

"Is that what he did?" Dad took a big spoonful of meat and potatoes. "Hmm?"

No, he hadn't. In fact, Rhett never even hinted that he might have feelings for me. The only reason we ended up getting close was because of my stupid idea to save Christmas by faking a relationship. Even if it was one of my worst ideas ever, I still believed our efforts did give the town hope. It brought us all together to make this holiday season the best ever.

I didn't regret kissing Rhett. Or spending two amazing nights with him. I supposed I was hurt because he couldn't choose me. Of course, if he had, I would've felt like the worst human being ever for making him pick me over his family.

My gaze shifted to Dad. Given the same set of circumstances, I would've made the same choice as Rhett. But for reasons I couldn't quite understand, I didn't want to forgive him and pretend he didn't almost marry another woman. My blood boiled every time I thought of Rhett and Sofia together. For a whole week, I did nothing but picture the two of them naked.

"That's the door, Sugarplum." Dad pointed to the foyer. "It might be him. I know Rhett very well. He won't stop coming over until you hear him out."

"Fine. I'll just kindly remind him that hell hasn't frozen over." I pushed off the bar stool and headed to the door with my heart up in my throat.

I pictured his dazzling blue yes, his dark hair, and that frustratingly irresistible smirk of his. Why did he have to be so Rhett? So perfect for me?

No, I couldn't go there anymore. I hated Rhett with all my soul. I swung the door open. "I don't ever want to see you again. Do you understand?"

"Um." Timmy, my ten-year-old neighbor glanced up at me with tears brimming his eyes.

"Omigod, Timmy. I'm so sorry. I thought you were someone else. Um." I put my hand on his shoulder. "I didn't mean to scare you. Can I get you a hot chocolate with marshmallows and a candy cane."

"Okay." He beamed at me and strolled right in. "Hi, Mr. Mayor."

"Hey Timmy. What are you doing out and about this late?" Dad was already re-heating the hot chocolate I had made earlier.

"I have something for Parker." He dug his hand inside his

coat and produced a set of envelopes tied with a red ribbon like a Christmas present. "It's from your boyfriend." He placed them on the counter and slid the mug Dad set in front of him a little closer so he could slurp on it.

"Rhett gave these to you?" I picked them up as butterflies fluttered in my stomach.

"He said he was going to wait for you at the Olde Windsor." He sipped from his drink.

"Right now?" I asked.

"Tomorrow."

"Tell him not to waste his time. I'm not meeting him anywhere." I crossed my arms over my chest.

"Okay." Dad ambled around the kitchen counter, using his crutches like he'd had them forever. "How about you go upstairs and rest. I'll get Timmy home." He ushered me toward the stairs.

"Okay." I hugged the letters to my chest and went to my bedroom.

I had not thought about Rhett's letter in eighteen years. Looking at the envelopes in my hand, I knew they would match the one letter I kept from Rhett. Wiping my cheek, I stood in front of my chest of drawers for several breaths before I pulled the drawer and rummaged through my socks to get the trinket box tucked in the back.

The tears streamed down my cheek as I plopped myself down on my bed and flipped open the box. I had a bunch of items in there that I had collected while in school— the charm bracelet I wore for years because Rowena gave it to me, movie stubs, an old candy cane, a picture of mom, and Rhett's letter neatly folded.

Parker,

I saw you at the cemetery today. You looked so sad because of your mom. My grandfather's driver wouldn't let me go to you. But I have a plan to ditch him tomorrow. If you're there, I'll come see you. I promise. You don't have to go alone.

Your friend,

Rhett

Droplets pelted on the Windsor letterhead and Rhett's squiggly writing. I thought of that day when Rhett sat with me by Mom's grave. He just sat there and let me cry my eyes out.

I shifted my attention to the stack of letters Timmy had delivered. Pulling at the ribbon, I let the envelopes scatter on the bed. What did it mean? Why would Rhett write more letters and not send them to me? My chest hurt to think that over the years, Rhett had so much to say to me and never felt he could.

My hands trembled as I opened the first one. The writing was still that of a ten-year-old. He wrote it the day he moved to California. In it, he promised he would come back, that he would never forget about me. He begged me not to forget him either.

"I never forgot about you, Rhett." I reached for the next letter.

It was dated a year later. He hated California because his mom was sad all the time. He wanted me to know that he was still thinking about me. And that he was coming back soon. In his next correspondence, he was ecstatic because he was finally coming home. And his grandfather had agreed to let him go to Old Town High so he could be with me.

In another letter, he invited me to prom. He was so mad when I went with Joe instead. He wrote again to share that he had been accepted to Columbia, and then Harvard Law. As the years went by, his writing began to look like the one I knew today, articulate and a little grumpy.

By the time I got to the last letter, my face looked like a punching bag from all the crying. And I was sure I sounded like a mad woman, answering his written questions, laughing at his crazy antics, and then crying that I wasn't there to share it all with him.

I opened the piece of paper and read. I stared at his last sentence until I couldn't see through my tears.

"I decided to run for Mayor. If I don't win, at least that would give me an opportunity to be with you for a little while before I go away for good. Winterstorm Village and you will always be the dream."

Sometime during the night, I fell into a deep sleep, tired from crying and numb from feeling too much. When I woke up, the sun was already shining through my window.

"Rhett." I jumped out of bed and headed straight for the bathroom to get ready.

As much as I wanted to see Rhett, I didn't want him to see me in the state of disarray I was in. I rushed out of the house with my hair still a little damp and my heart thrashing in my throat. I had no doubt Rhett would be waiting for me by the clock tower, or what little was left of it. I knew he'd be there because he'd always been there, fighting to stay with me. Always.

I turned the corner on main street and spotted him immediately. He froze when he saw me, visibly tensed and heart broken. When I beamed at him, he relaxed and stuffed his hands in the pockets of his trousers, looking hotter than I remembered. Being apart this past week had been hell. I never wanted to be without him. Not ever again.

"You read them." He smiled at the ground then glanced up. "All the letters I never sent."

"I did." I closed the space between us.

"I was afraid you wouldn't show." He brushed the pad of his thumb over my jawline. "Parker, I'm so sorry for starting something with you that I knew I couldn't commit to. I had wanted you for so long. I wanted to keep the fantasy going for as long as I could. It was so selfish of me."

"You did the right thing. You wouldn't be the man I love if you hadn't chosen your family. Too many people depended on you." I had to admit that maybe my ego had played a big part in me wanting Rhett to choose me over Sofia.

"Say that again." He nuzzled my neck. "Say you love me."

"I love you, Rhett Windsor. I think I've always loved you." I hugged him tight. "Even when I thought you were the most stubborn and infuriating man I'd ever met."

"I love you too, Parker Cruz. I'm done saying goodbye." He pressed his forehead to mine. "Do you forgive me? From here on out, there's only you. I swear that to you. No more marriage contracts."

"I do. It's all in the past now." I threw my arms around his neck.

He wrapped his arms around my waist, picked me up and turned a half circle. Across the street, Sam and Rowena stood outside the bakery shop beaming at us. As I looked around the town square, I realized we were not alone.

"Should we go somewhere else?" I whispered in his ear.

He peered over my head, then chuckled. "Can I take you home?"

"Dad is staying with me for a few days." I gripped the lapels of his heavy coat. "I missed you."

"My place then?" He flashed me a sexy smile that made all kinds of dirty promises. "I'm back at the mansion." He gestured toward the limo parked on the other side of the street.

"Are you trying to seduce me with limo rides?"

"The thought did cross my mind." He ran the backs of his fingers over my cheek. "I was ready to do whatever it took to get you back."

"Including baring your soul to me with those old letters?" I asked as he pulled me toward him and ushered me to his limo.

"Yeah." He kissed the top of my head.

"Home, sir?" A very serious driver opened the door for us.

"Yes, Louis. We're going home." Rhett gestured for me to get in, then climbed in behind me.

The door shut and the whole world fell away.

"Bennett and Sofia, huh? I can't believe she's pregnant." I asked when the limo peeled off the curb. "I saw them making out at the hospital. I wonder if she was there to take a pregnancy test? That would make sense. It would've been risky to do it at home."

"Why didn't you tell me?" He shifted his body to face me.

"I don't know. I didn't want to be the jealous ex-girlfriend." I placed my palm to his handsome face. "I was going insane thinking about the two of you together."

"I never touched her." He reached for my waist and pulled me toward him until I straddled his lap. "I've never wanted anyone else but you."

He captured my mouth. His searing kiss tasted like home to me. I tunneled my fingers through his hair and deepened our kiss as I removed my heavy coat. I wanted him so badly.

"I've never had sex in a limo before," I confessed on his lips.

"We'll have to remedy that." He gripped my butt and scooted me up so I sat firmly on his erection.

"Hmmm, I missed this." I moaned softly, pressing my lips to his.

His tongue plunged inside my mouth as he rocked his hips into my mound. I glanced down at my chunky sweater, leggings and boots. Not the best outfit for limo sex. As if he could read my mind, he leaned forward to remove my shoes while he unbuckled his belt to free his cock.

In five seconds flat, with his mouth still on mine, he relieved me of my leggings and underwear. Oh yeah, this man was trouble. I didn't care that I was half naked in the back of his limo. All I knew was that I wanted him inside me in the worst way possible.

I panted a breath as a surge of adrenaline and desire burned through my body like tiny timbers. His coat came off next, along with his button-down shirt. Running my hands down his muscled chest, I kissed his heated skin.

"You are so beautiful." He cupped my neck and brought me down for a kiss. His shaft pressed against my entrance for a breath, then slowly pushed through my wet folds. "So good. Mine."

"Yes." I let my head fall back to savor the pleasure radiating from my core. "How much time do we have?"

Rhett let go of my breast to hit a button on the overhead console. "Louis, change of plans. Just drive."

"Yes, sir," Louis responded immediately.

"There." Rhett guided my hips to deepen our connection,

sending a shock of rapture through me. "We have all the time in the world, Parker."

Thank you so much for reading LIKE IT'S CHRISTMAS. I hope you enjoyed Rhett and Parker's holiday story. If you did, please consider leaving a review. Reviews help other readers like you find my books.

Have you met Henry Cavalier yet? RELEASE YOU is a second chance, a grumpy x sunshine billionaire romance with all the spice.

DOWNLOAD Nikki and Henry's love story TODAY!

. . .

If you like your billionaires a little darker, check out
King of Beasts, a powerful retelling of Beauty and the Beast.

Download KING OF BEASTS Today!

WHAT's next in the Winterstorm Village Series? Thor and Briar's story is coming soon in this best friend's older brother Christmas novel.

Add to your Goodreads TBR so you don't miss the release.

www.ingramcontent.com/pod-product-compliance
Lightning Source LLC
Chambersburg PA
CBHW060710190726
48289CB00002B/624

9 781949 760811